Where Am I Now—When I Need Me?

WHERE

AM I NOW-

WHEN I

NEED ME?

by GEORGE

AXELROD

NEW YORK / THE VIKING PRESS

For Is Dretzin

PROLOGUE

1

This is a suicide note.

A journal, if nothing more, of these last days.

It will, I fear, drag on for a time, as, alas, I shall pull no trigger. Not only would my courage fail me at that final, consummate moment of despair, but my wife Margery is Chairman of the Sane Gun Law Committee of Westport, Connecticut, and as an example of her good citizenship is insisting that I turn over to the Westport police my World War II German P-38. It is rusty, of course, and to my knowledge has not once been fired in joy, much less in anger.

But it has its uses. Often in the cocktail twilight of a summer's evening I break it out and arouse one or more of the bare-midriffed wives of my neighbors with the tale of how I had, in the Ardennes Forest, stooped and plucked the thing from the holster of my fallen victim, usually an SS Colonel. *God, Harvey, it's so hard to think of you as a soldier! Mike never got any nearer to anything than Bush Terminal in Brooklyn!* Pause. Always, the pause. Then: *What* (asks Bare-midriffed-wife-of-neighbor, now sexually inflamed by the mystery that lurks behind my disillusioned eyes; eyes that have perhaps seen too much) *does it really feel like to kill a man?*

3

The easy shrug. The funny, twisted smile. The turning away, not wishing to speak of it. The reaching once again for the shaker.

Actually, I bought it (my rusted but still, I hope, lethal German P-38) in the summer of 1945 from a drunken Air Force T/5 for a carton of Chesterfields, which he, in turn, exchanged for a brief ejaculation and an extended and extremely painful case of clap. Maybe I will not turn it in, after all. Maybe I will simply lock it in the filing cabinet here in my office. Margery will never know.

* * * * *

Sleeping pills are out of the question. I would, I know, take either too few or too many and simply wake some hours later in a semi-private room, trembling with nausea and disgrace.

* * * * *

I have a fear of high places.

* * * * *

And if one wished to drown oneself at Pebble Beach (having no pool of one's own and being too well-mannered to embarrass a more affluent neighbor), one would have to walk out at least a quarter of a mile over a nasty, pebbled bottom, and then one would still be only waist-deep in slightly polluted water.

Nevertheless, I am dying.

Slowly.

But by my own hand.

This is a suicide note.

* * * * *

My name is Harvey Bernstein. I am forty-six years old. I am a failed writer; author of three novels, two volumes of poetry, and perhaps four hundred book reviews, all of absurd books, reviewed for absurd publications. My stomach hurts in the morning. I have a bottle of vodka hidden in my desk at the office. I am employed as an instructor at THE BEST-SELLING WRITERS SCHOOL in nearby Condon Heights, Connecticut. None of my three novels was best-selling. My two volumes of poetry sold not at all. My four hundred book reviews were all unfavorable.

My son Bruce is at Berkeley. He sends me letters from time to time when there is trouble with the carburetor. My daughter Linda is a freshman at Barnard where she is living, off-campus, with Lester, a graduate student in African Literature. As there is no African Literature to speak of, his time is very much his own. And Linda's. She brought him home to dinner last night. *Guess who's coming to dinner?* I guessed. Margery was beside herself in a kind of ecstasy. *We have not failed her! We have not failed her!* was her war cry throughout the horrid Sunday afternoon.

Lester is very black indeed. Toward the end of the evening he twice addressed me as "baby" in what I took to be the pejorative sense. Otherwise, he was pleasant enough. And, I suppose, in a way, attractive. More attractive than Linda, surely, who is, when it comes right down to it, a rather fuzzy-looking girl.

Where, I wonder, are the tall girls, with long, suntanned legs and blond hair flying, that I dreamed of in my youth?

*   *   *   *   *

I awoke this morning filled with the knowledge of impending death. It was raining. It has been raining for a week. My dreams had been of blue water and sun-drenched beaches and tall girls with long, sun-tanned legs and blond hair flying, running toward me in slow motion in the manner of deodorant commercials on the television.

Cold, gusty wind drove the rain against the bedroom windows. Margery, thank God, was still asleep when I left the house. My stomach hurt, but I have mentioned that before. I drove (through gusts and rain) to the office.

The office, THE BEST-SELLING WRITERS SCHOOL of Condon Heights, Connecticut, is a one-story edifice of glass and steel, divided, within, into cubicles where we, the instructors, instruct by mail under artificial light.

Before me on the plastic surface of my desk lay the latest installment of the novel by Mrs. Edna Mortimer (housewife); a new chapter in the memoirs of General Harrison Bradley (USA, Ret.); a sonnet (part, I regret to say, of an extended sequence) by Charles Douglas Potter (hairdresser), plus numerous less ambitious exercises by students not so advanced as Mrs. Mortimer, the General, and Charles Douglas Potter.

My secretary, Miss Akron (whose name falsely suggests a beauty contest winner), has just brought in the morning mail. Applications from prospective students. Each will contain a filled-in questionnaire and a sample of the applicant's prose. Twenty-three of them this morning. God help me!

*   *   *   *   *

Mrs. Mortimer's latest chapter describes the seduction of her heroine, a movie star ineptly based on the character of the late Marilyn Monroe, at the hands of a Jewish psychiatrist. Jacqueline Susann and Phil Roth will have a lot to answer for when they finally reach that Great Lending Library In The Sky.

*   *   *   *   *

6

It is raining even harder now. I think I shall add a stab of vodka to the instant coffee Miss Akron has just placed before me. Then, on to Mrs. Mortimer and the seduction of Jacqueline Susann by Philip Roth. At least Mr. Roth refers to it as "pussy." Mrs. Mortimer speaks of it as "her pulsating virginia."

Self-pity overwhelms me.

The General has been given his first command. A post in Alaska. Alaska is an American Territory situated on the northwestern edge of the Continent, he observes. He is thrilled and looks forward to a winter of high adventure. Mr. Potter's sonnet (as usual) celebrates the Grecian glories of the male body.

Someday, perhaps, I shall open an envelope and out of it will fall . . .

2

THE BEST-SELLING WRITERS SCHOOL
Condon Heights, Conn.

APPLICATION FORM AND LITERARY
APTITUDE TEST

(Please answer all questions. If more space is required, answers should be typed, double space, on standard 8½″ x 11″ typing paper, using one side of the sheet only. If, in our opinion, your application shows that you have genuine aptitude for writing, you will be assigned to one of our instructors, all of whom, by the way, are themselves professional best-selling writers. Your application will be processed as rapidly as possible and you will be hearing from us in a very few days. Good luck!)

(1) NAME: Cathy. I'm a girl with only a first name. The last names I make up to suit the occasion. Lewis. Lovibond. Lombard. Lamont. Choose one. And even the first name changes from time to time and season to season.

(2) ADDRESS: Cities. New York. L.A. Vegas. Miami. Choose one. If I pass this test you can reach me, if you move swiftly, at 42931 Northern Boulevard, Astoria, Long Island. I share Apartment 4D with Joanne. Also a girl with only a first name. That, too, subject to change without notice. When we first met, she was Rhoda and I was Eugenie. I think my named showed greater imagination.

(3) AGE: 18. 19. 20. 21. 22. 23. 24. Choose one. Joanne (Rhoda) is the same age.

(4) BANK: I'm sorry but I do not have a bank. I suppose a Best-Selling Writer should have a bank, but I am not a Best-Selling Writer yet,

although I am keeping fingers, toes, etc.
crossed! I am enclosing five one-hundred-
dollar bills (in case I pass the test). If it
is more, just write and let me know how much.
If it is less, you can send me the change. Is
that all right? Joanne put money in a bank
once to get the dishes and the toaster. Then
she started getting letters from the tax
department and we had to move. I told her if
she wanted dishes and a toaster she should
go to a store where they sell dishes and
toasters. Not to a bank. Be sure and let me
know if it is more and I will send the correct
amount by return mail.

(5) PRESENT OCCUPATION: "Model," which is of
course a euphemism. Did I spell that right? I
have no dictionary at the moment. If I pass
the test I will buy one. Which do you
recommend? There are so many. Actually, I
have done some modeling from time to time.
See enclosed photograph.

PHOTOGRAPH

(6) EXPLAIN IN 100 WORDS WHAT YOU HOPE TO
TO ACHIEVE BY TAKING THIS COURSE. (Use separate sheet as explained in the instructions above.)

SEPARATE SHEET 1

"WHAT I HOPE TO ACHIEVE BY TAKING THIS
COURSE"

What an ass-hole question! I hope to
become a best-selling writer. Why else would
I be taking this course? I'm sorry. I didn't
mean to be vulgar, but it (Question 6) is so
silly that I didn't know what to answer.
Actually, I think questions are more important
than answers. For example, does a word like
ass-hole which has a hyphen count as one
word or two? That is the sort of thing I hope
to learn. And where to begin. That's another
problem. I was born . . . I awoke . . . He
plunged it into me . . . All excellent
beginnings. But which one? (100 words)

(7) TO TEST YOUR LITERARY ABILITY, PLEASE
WRITE A FIVE-HUNDRED-WORD ESSAY ON THE
TOPIC: THE SINGLE MOST TRANSCENDING EX-
PERIENCE OF MY LIFE. (Please use separate sheet or
sheets as explained above.)

SEPARATE SHEET 2

"THE SINGLE MOST TRANSCENDING EXPERI-
ENCE OF MY LIFE"

The single most transcending experience of
my life occurred in Webb City, Mo. when I was
sixteen years old. As a young girl I was very
ugly because of my nose (which I inherited
from Grandpa who was known far and wide as
Captain Hook not because he was a captain of
anything) and my hair which was kind of
no-color and somewhat kinky. Not kinky like
we use it today such as making it with boots
and electric toothbrushes etc. Just all tight
and curly and sweaty in summer. Anyway I was
really stacked from the age of eleven on but
it did me no good because of my nose and hair
etc. At the time I had a big thing about a boy
named Harold something I have forgotten his
name who was in my class. He would not even
look at me of course because of my nose and
hair etc. He saw me in a bathing suit at the
4th of July picnic and said in my hearing that
if he could wrap an American Flag over my head
so that he did not have to look at my nose and
hair etc. he would consider throwing me one
for Old Glory. Do you have to put quotation
marks if he said it but you are just telling
it? Anyway, Grandpa died (of drink) and my
share was $600 so against the wishes of my
mother who wanted the money for herself to
open a Charm and Tap Dancing School I took the
$600 and went to K.C. (by bus) and bought
myself a nose job. There was enough left over
so I could get my hair bleached (suicide blond
was the shade I chose) and straightened and
be fitted for a contraceptive device. That was
before the pill. Can you imagine? It seems

like the Dark Ages! Anyway believe me it was
worth the $600 and one week to the day or night
actually from when the bandages came off I was
in the back seat of Harold's Chevy. At the big
moment for him (personally I didn't feel much
of anything as my left leg was wrapped around
his neck and had fallen asleep) he whispered
for me to say the dirtiest word I knew. Eager
to oblige, as I am to this very day, I did so.
What I said was ointment. I still think
ointment is the dirtiest word I know but I
realize now that I am more experienced in such
things that was probably not the word he had
in mind. Not only that but he probably thought
I was making an insulting reference to his
skin condition which was not so hot and he had
to keep putting this stuff on it although
only at night which didn't matter to me as he
was built great and very handsome except for
his skin condition. Anyway he was so upset
that he twisted loose and came all over my
(500 words)

3

THE BEST-SELLING WRITERS SCHOOL
Condon Heights, Conn.

Miss Cathy Lewis Lovibond Lombard Lamont
Apartment 4D
42931 Northern Boulevard
Astoria, Long Island

Dear "Cathy":
    Very funny. I assume that "you" are one of
three persons. Max Wilk, Max Shulman, or Ed
Hotchner, all good friends and neighbors in the
Westport-Condon Heights area. What I can't
understand is why you would take the trouble to
do this to me! A practical joke I can understand.
But the lengths! Actually to send five (genuine!
I took the money to the bank myself—by the way
what would you like me to do with the clock-radio?)
one-hundred-dollar bills! What is the purpose?
What harm have I ever done you? I suppose, like
most writers you still bear a grudge (Grudges?
Perhaps the three of you are in this together!)
over reviews I have written of your various books
from time to time. But even so . . .
    All right. We've had a good laugh. I would be
interested, however, to know where you got the
photograph. Is she real? Is there such a girl? Do
you know her? Could I meet her? You see, you
bastards, your vicious, black practical joke has
worked. The seeds of doubt (or is it belief?)
have been planted. Five hundred dollars for a
practical joke? Very much out of character for
three internationally famous cheapskates like
you. I don't know. I don't know.
    Bruce's car has broken down altogether. This
time it has to do with the transmission. Four
hundred dollars is requested air-mail special.
Linda is still with the unspeakable schwartze.

Margery is going through (as she has been since
the day we were married twenty-two years ago)
change of life. I am, unlike yourselves, no longer
publishable. I am failed. I am vulnerable. This
is a suicide note.

But, my God, if there were such a girl! I
could teach her and mold her! ("And screw her," I
hear you dirty bastards chortling to each other
as you read this.) My life would be changed. There
would be a reason to get up in the morning and
drive to this hateful office and read and correct
all this hateful, untalented, hopeless prose.
Why does every asshole (asshole, by the way, is
not necessarily hyphenated) in the world think
he can write fiction? And why is it all, the
very worst of it, the dregs of it, inflicted
on me?

Frankly, Cathy, Max, Ed, Max, whoever you
are, I have a confession to make. I have already
been at the vodka bottle that I keep hidden in my
desk. I have had three belts plus the shot I
regularly sneak into Miss Akron's version of
instant coffee. It is still raining as it has been
for the last two weeks. I am, on this hateful
March morning, in the mood to believe.

Perhaps, Cathy, you are real!

But I must have proof! I will not, in my
precarious condition, devote the waning days of
my life to laboring over, struggling to correct,
struggling to improve a series of "lessons"
concocted amid roars of laughter, over drunken
lunches by my three so-called friends. Lessons
that will later be read aloud with ghoulish glee
at some unfortunate cocktail party. Very probably
with my wife and daughter and boogie soon-I-
fear-to-be (this is an interesting use of the
hyphen, forming as it does a compound adjective)
son-in-law present.

Max! Ed! Max! Don't do this to me! If it is

a joke, drop it now. You've made your point, whatever it might have been.

But, Cathy, if you are real, there is no limit !

You know life, I know grammar and sentence structure. Together we can own the world. I will teach you to become a best-selling writer. And you can teach me . . . what? I don't know. To live, I suppose. Or at least to want to. (Sometimes a sentence may be ended with a preposition but only for intentional dramatic effect.)

I am quite drunk now and it is only eleven-thirty-five. I have suddenly become very conscious of the hyphen. I, myself, tend to overuse it ; as I do the semicolon. It is rainy and cold here. As I stare morosely through the window at the flooded parking lot, I realize what it is I am actually dying of. I am dying of despair ! I will mail this myself, as I do not want Miss Akron to see it. And I wish to mail it before I have second thoughts.

Most sincerely,

(On my part and I
hope on yours)

Your Instructor
HB

4

Dear HB,

Of course, I am real. The photograph was taken two years ago and I have put on a pound or so since but only (so I am told) in the right places. I was glad to learn that asshole does not need a hyphen. You learn something new every day. I have never thought very much about the semicolon but that is interesting too. I'm sure you can teach me to become a best-selling writer.

You did not say in your letter whether or not I passed the test. As a matter of fact your letter sounded kind of crazy. You do not sound like a very happy person. But I guess most best-selling writers are unhappy and have a tendency to drink too much from time to time. I once spent a weekend with a best-selling writer (in Miami) and he drank the whole time. He also cried a lot. Afterwards I read two of his books (both best-sellers). They were very kinky (boots, electric toothbrushes etc.) but also very beautiful. I must say he wrote about it a lot better than he did it in real life. But probably he does it better when he is not pissed. Many people do.

Are you a best-selling writer? Have I ever read any of your books? Could you send me one or two? (I will pay for them of course.) Please write soon and tell me if I passed the test. And what you want me to do next. Will there be regular printed lessons or will you just write and tell me what to do?

> Your friend
> (and I hope student)
> CATHY

P.S. You can keep the clock-radio. I already have one that I got at a store where they sell clock-radios. Not at a bank.

5

I ran into Max Wilk at a cocktail party two nights ago. Shulman, he tells me, is in Hollywood; Hotchner is in Europe, so that, more or less, rules *them* out. I dropped several not-too-veiled hints about prostitutes with literary ambitions and an unlimited supply of hundred-dollar bills. He looked at me blankly, clearly assuming I was drunk. Since he no longer drinks (gout), he assumes that everyone else is drunk at all times. He has a new novel. I have been asked to review it for the *Diners' Club Magazine*. I reviewed Phil Roth's first book for the *Partisan Review*. Now I am dying and unpublishable (except by the *Diners' Club Magazine*) in Westport. Where are the golden girls of my dreams? Where are the reviews by Roth of *my* new novels? Oh, God! Perhaps Ed Hotchner will review my suicide note. For *Popular Mechanics*.

* * * * *

I have locked "Cathy's" photograph in the drawer where I keep the vodka. Last night, shortly after the eleven-o'clock news, Margery turned insanely amorous. It was not a happy occasion. I had already taken my pills. She had already done whatever it is she does to herself at night that makes her look rather as she does in the daytime only more so. I could not for the life of me get it up. Then I thought of Cathy. The effect was extraordinary. I have not performed with such style in years. I found myself suddenly thinking "kinky" thoughts. I am toying with the idea of obtaining an electric toothbrush. How in God's name, I wonder, does one employ such an instrument sexually? At the moment of climax I murmured the word "ointment" into Margery's ear plug. (She had, in her sudden passion, forgotten to remove them.) Very satisfactory. Of course, like so many best-selling writers, I was pissed.

But I am not a best-selling writer. I am a forty-six-year-old drunken failure.

Later, sitting alone in the dark in the breakfast nook with a vodka and Fresca, I cried.

* * * * *

It is still raining. The General finds his new post near Juneau, Alaska (an American Territory in the northeastern corner of the Continent), disappointing. But there is, he writes, an ample supply of whiskey at the officers' mess. He is grateful for small blessings.

Mrs. Mortimer's heroine Madelene's virginia (sic) continues to pulsate (sic) merrily. Sick. (Me.) Albert, the subject of Mr. Potter's sonnet sequence, continues to bulge provocatively at the crotch of his jeans. He (Mr. Potter) unfortunately chooses to rhyme "provocatively" with "sock it to me" as the final couplet of Sonnet 163.

* * * * *

This is a suicide note.

* * * * *

I must make a decision. Either Cathy is real or she isn't. If she is (have I misjudged the whole matter? Are Max and Ed and Max innocent? Could this be a practical joke devised by Phil Roth and Miss Susann?), then I must answer her letter. I must begin her course of instruction. I have the clock-radio on my desk. But it does not work, as it runs on batteries which the bank failed to supply. Cathy is right. Banks should stay out of merchandising.

* * * * *

She is (I have made my decision) awaiting, with pulsating virginia, my answer. Astoria (as an address) is beyond the inventive powers of any of the aforementioned best-selling assholes. I (frankly) have no idea if asshole should be hyphenated or not. But as an instructor of creative writing I must take a firm (if not bulging) position. I shall write her in a moment or two. As soon as I sneak another look/drink from my locked drawer.

* * * * *

God, she is beautiful. Can she be real?
I believe! I believe! I believe!
I believe in the stork! I believe in Santa Claus! I believe in God! I believe in the fucking Easter Bunny!
I believe in Cathy Lewis Lovibond Lombard Lamont!

* * * * *

Harvey Bernstein (I have begun to think of myself in the third person; a sign, I have read, of impending madness) opens his desk drawer.

He takes out the vodka bottle and places it shamelessly before him on the desk. He takes out the photograph. He studies it, thinking kinky thoughts, until the crotch of his baggy gray flannels bulges as provocatively as the jeans of Mr. Potter's Albert.

He takes a belt from the neck of the bottle. He reaches for a sheet of paper, inserts it into his typewriter, and begins to tap the keys.

* * * * *

Dear Cathy,
Good news!
You have passed the test!
It is very important for a writer who wishes to become a best-selling author to choose a subject with which he or she is familiar. As your life appears to be a most interesting one, I think we might begin by having you continue with your autobiography, starting at the point where

you left off in your most interesting five-
hundred-word essay. . . .

*   *   *   *   *

The letter itself ran thirteen pages, growing (I fear) more incoherent as he consumed vodka; and passion, in turn, consumed him. His concluding sentence was "I love you." Which I hope I had the sense to X out before mailing, but I do not remember.

I am forty-six years old. I drink in the mornings. I am in love with an 18, 19, 20, 21, 22, 23, 24 (choose one)-year-old prostitute whom I have never met.

This way surely leads to the self-destruction I so desperately seek.

The auto-da-fé has begun.

But it will take some time for the flames to consume me.

(Suicide note to be continued)

Chapter **O N E**

1

"Out of your mother-grabbing mind," Joanne said as she wandered in from the bathroom, drying her hair with a large, mascara-stained towel. Joanne, formerly Rhoda and before that God knows what, had been considered for most of her life a dumb, rather sexy-looking blonde. As she had recently changed her hair color, she was now generally regarded as a dumb, rather sexy-looking brunette.

Cathy found her roommate's stupidity essentially soothing.

One of the things that amused and soothed her most about Joanne was Joanne's absolute refusal to accept the fact that they were both prostitutes.

"*Prostitute?*" a recent argument had run. "Wednesday night Martin let me into the Côte in a pants suit. Do you think he'd let some cheap hooker in there with a *pants suit?* A headwaiter like Martin is a great judge of *people!* He *has* to be! That's his *thing!* Judging people. Judging like who should get the right table. Judging like are they good for the check. Shit like that. So if I *was* a prostitute, don't you think Martin would be the first one to know it?"

So touched was Cathy by this line of reasoning that she

politely refrained from pointing out that while her roommate had, indeed, been admitted to the Côte d'Azur in a pants suit, she had been admitted as a member of a party of six, the host being a world-famous movie star whom that excellent judge of character, Martin, judged (correctly) to have arrived at the door at a pitch of drunkenness likely to explode into violence at any moment. As the interior of the restaurant had been recently and expensively redecorated, admitting, without argument, a cheap, pants-suited hooker seemed very much the wisest course of action.

What neither of them knew was that when the movie star called for a reservation the following night he was politely but firmly told there was no table available. And that he would be told the same thing every time he called till his dying day or until his mania reached such a point that he decided to buy the place. It was incidents like this that had caused him to wind up owning half a dozen fashionable restaurants both here and abroad. Three of these were so ludicrously successful that they had very nicely offset some considerable oil losses sustained during the star's previous fiscal year. Which, in turn, had annoyed his accountants, whose tax plan it had been to use the oil losses to offset his company's unexpected surplus of nonrental income. Actually it turned out to be just about a wash.

*   *   *   *   *

"In what way?" Cathy asked.

"In what way what?"

"In what way am I out of my mother-grabbing mind? Incidentally, did you know that 'mother-grabbing' is a hyphenated compound adjective and about ten years out-of-date?"

Joanne looked blank. It was an expression that became her.

The rainy spell that had lasted through most of March

and April had ended, giving way to unseasonable heat and leaden skies, sullen with humidity.

It was six o'clock in the evening.

Cathy was seated, naked, at a card table on which a portable typewriter had been placed. It was Cathy's decision to forgo an evening of fun and profit with a famous movie director and his producer, who were in from the Coast to scout locations in Harlem for an updated version of *Anna Karenina* which they planned to shoot with an all-black cast, that had prompted Joanne's original remark. She fluffed her hair now with the towel.

"All right, then, if you don't like 'out of your mother-grabbing mind,' how does 'I think you're absolutely bonkers' grab you?"

Joanne was inordinately pleased with "bonkers," a phrase she had recently picked up from a visiting English jockey, who had paid her in American dollars from an illegal account kept here under his mother(an American)'s name.

"I have work to do," Cathy said. "I'm getting behind in my assignments again."

She rolled a new sheet of paper into the typewriter. She was anxious to get on with becoming a best-selling writer. But it was impossible to work while Joanne put clothes on and took them off again, dumping them on the floor and complaining about her weight.

Joanne's bosoms, while not misshapen, were enormous. At the moment they were a great professional asset. But when they went they would go fast.

A decision was finally made.

A green pants suit. Joanne had an extensive wardrobe of pants suits.

"What if they want to eat first? What if they want to go to a decent restaurant?"

"We can always go to the Côte," Joanne said haughtily.

The heat in the apartment was oppressive. They had talked about putting in air-conditioning but it meant running in two-twenty lines and they had never quite got around to it.

"This place is like a steam bath," Cathy said. She rose from her typist's chair (newly purchased from an office-supply firm on Lexington Avenue) and went to the window. It stuck a little but she finally managed to force it open. She stood for a moment leaning out over the sill, breathing in whatever there was to breathe and watching the lights flicker on in the hideous rabbit-warren apartment buildings that lined the boulevard.

"Are they sending a car or what?" she asked, not bothering to look back over her shoulder. At least the carbon monoxide billowing up from the street was fresh carbon monoxide.

"They said to take a cab. They're *using* the car. They're looking for *locations*. They're not here for *pleasure!*"

Joanne talked largely in italics, which was another thing Cathy found soothing.

Then Cathy noticed the man.

He was standing on the sidewalk directly across from the apartment. He was staring up at the window. The light was still good enough for her to see him clearly. He was forty-six or -seven. (She had become terribly good at guessing men's ages. It was a parlor trick she sometimes did for side bets. They, if they took the bet, would always have to show their driver's licenses. That was part of the deal. Sometimes, when they were lying about their names, they didn't want to show their driver's licenses. In that case she collected by default. She was, however, almost always right.) He, the man on the sidewalk staring up, was neither good-looking nor bad. In fact he had no particular look at all. His eyes were hidden by huge glasses. For all she knew they were twin telescopes—one, she suddenly realized, trained directly at her left tit, the other at her right. That is, if they *were* twin telescopes. Maybe the poor bastard was blind as a bat and simply looking for an address or something. He wore a tweed jacket and gray baggy trousers. He seemed harmless enough.

He could, of course, be the person who would subsequently be known in the world press as "The Astoria Strangler," just standing there, bracing himself for his first shot. But Cathy doubted it. She decided to play it another way.

She waved. Not a wave with any invitation even remotely implied. Just a simple "hi-there" wave. Then she rubbed her hands slowly over her breasts, lingeringly jiggling her thumbs on each nipple.

On the street, the man turned and fled. Some strangler.

From behind her Joanne said, "What are you *doing* standing in the window with your *knockers* hanging out! This whole *place* is absolutely *creeping* with *sex* maniacs! Didn't you see *The Boston Strangler?* Now come on, get in here and pull the blind! *You* may want to be *murdered* and *raped* and *strangled* in your bed, but *I* certainly *don't!*"

"We ought to put in air-conditioning," Cathy said, turning away from the window. "It's like a steam bath in here."

"There's air-conditioning at the Plaza," Joanne said, slipping her blue plastic diaphragm container into her purse. She had no faith in the pill as a method of contraception. In addition she claimed that it caused her skin to break out.

"How do you know you won't be murdered, raped, and strangled where you're going?" Cathy asked, reseating herself at the card table.

"At the *Plaza* Hotel? In *New York City?* With two gentlemen who are here from the *Coast* to look for *locations?* Are you out of your mother-grabbing mind?"

Pretty soon she was gone. Cathy watched from the window until she was safely in a cab. There was no sign of the man with the twin-telescope spectacles.

2

The silence was refreshing. So was the lack of italics. Cathy picked up the latest communiqué from her instructor. HB, if that's how he liked to refer to himself. Maybe that was one of the rules of the School or something. That the instructors be known to their students only by their initials. Bull shit.

Harvey Bernstein.

She knew his name as well as he did. Better, probably, judging from the hysterical nature of his more recent letters. The poor bastard seemed to be having a terrible identity problem. With no technical psychiatric background Cathy understood the nature of the identity problem as well as anyone in the United States with the possible exception of Lawrence S. Kubie, M.D. ("Neurotic Distortion of the Creative Process"; Porter Lectures, Series 22, University of Kansas Press, 1958).

After all, she was, as she had put it herself, a girl with no last name. Frequently, on tricks, she would even forget the first name she happened to be using. And she had made up so many different backgrounds and ages for herself that she was no longer able to distinguish between what had actually happened in her life and what she imagined had happened. Maybe there was very little difference, since imagining is also a form of happening. But Cathy was unconcerned with such high-level abstractions.

A drop of sweat, dripping from her chin to the upper portion of her left breast and then, still unnoticed, puddling down the soft pink skin slope, leaped from her nipple and landed squarely in the middle of the typed page that she had prepared the night before as part of her new assignment for HB.

It left a stain.

It (the stain) caused her no distress. Instead she smiled. On Harvey's last letter there had also been a stain. He had handled it brilliantly. He had simply ringed the stain with a pencil and written in his own hand: tear-drop, from right eye. She now picked up a pencil, ringed *her* stain, and wrote in her own hand: sweat-drop from left tit.

She only hoped that the mark of her tit-drop (she liked that better, but it was too late to rewrite it without messing up the page) would not turn the poor bugger on even more than he seemed to be already. Maybe she should never have sent him the photograph. But, knowing she was barely literate and wanting desperately to take the course, she had done what she had always done. Used what she had.

Two weeks before, he had sent her a paperback edition of one of his (it now turned out, non-best-selling) novels. He had been very careful of course. He had torn off the cover and the title page, thereby hoping (or not hoping?) to keep his identity secret. What he had (or had not) forgotten was that the title of the non-best-seller was printed on the top of each page.

It had been a simple matter to go to the public library, check the title in the card files, discover the author's name and, after obtaining a library card under a name she could no longer remember, take out his other two novels and his two volumes of poetry.

The novels seemed more or less to celebrate the use of the hyphen and the semicolon and had to do with rivalries among professors on various college campuses. Bull shit.

But the poetry was something else. She had never encountered blank verse before. Between it and his letters, he had managed somehow to touch her.

The truth of the matter was that Cathy had developed a kind of long-distance crush on him. She had always been a sucker for losers. Especially born losers.

The prose passage she was working on now was a description of her life as a performer in blue movies. Most of it was nonsense, of course. She *had* done a lot of nude posing and had made a few stag reels in California when she first got there.

The stag reels were no big deal.

She had been living with the boy she screwed on film anyway. And she'd banged the director-cameraman a couple of times before she'd even met the leading man. But, for Harvey's benefit, she was making it sound as glamorous as possible.

A small but beautifully equipped studio hidden away in the Hollywood Hills. Dressing rooms with the performer's name on the door.

"At that time," she was writing when the phone rang, "Jigger and I were at the peak of our success. We were considered by many to be the Jeanette MacDonald and Nelson Eddy of the stag film industry."

She *was* trying to turn the poor bastard on. No question. Then the bloody telephone. How can a writer really create when the bloody phone keeps ringing all the time?

Naturally, it was Joanne.

Naturally, it was a crisis.

Naturally, she had taken the wrong diaphragm case. The empty one. Could Cathy please just jump into a cab and bring the right one, on the *top* shelf of the medicine cabinet, to Suite 1867–8 at the Plaza Hotel? The pants suit had been just fine. They had had dinner in the room. Is a pants suit all right, she had asked. No pants would be even better, had been the reply. And that was how it had gone. Until the blue plastic case proved to be empty. Terribly sorry. Just jump in a cab. The boys from the Coast were absolutely charming. One (the director) was even kind of good-looking. Very young and groovy. In addition to which (the director was on the bedroom extension himself by now) the film they were seeking locations for was a very important film indeed and would very probably make an important statement about the Negro condition. From a White Russian's point of view, of course. But then Pushkin, a very important Russian writer, had been a boogie himself, and on and on like that. Anyway, they'd love to have her come up if only just for a drink as one of the girls they'd asked was having her period or something and had dropped out.

What the hell. It was hot in the apartment. The suite in the Plaza was air-conditioned. She was getting bored sitting here alone writing lies about the blue-movie business.

And Harvey Bernstein was such a chicken shit that he wouldn't even tell her his real name.

She was getting dressed when the phone rang again.

Could she also bring the stuff? Not the whole jar or anything like that. Just enough for maybe half a dozen joints. Okay. Why not?

I tried, she thought, I tried.

She looked at her tit-drop-stained page and figured, as so many best-selling writers had before her, why not have a little fun tonight? There's always tomorrow to get it written. In a curious way she was on the right track.

Harvey Bernstein, lurking in the shadows across from her apartment, watched her get into the cab. Since taking flight he had drunk five martinis in a bar up the street. It was only after her cab had turned the corner that he got the idea of breaking into her apartment.

Chapter T W O

1

The younger one, the director, *was* kind of groovy, and the producer, while less attractive, had a wang the size of Nashua's (winner in 1955 of the Preakness and the Belmont Stakes. Swaps copped the Derby that year). By the time Cathy arrived, the three of them were seated, stark naked, on the floor amid the remains of an expensive room-service dinner, playing spin the bottle.

The air-conditioner was going full blast.

Cathy insisted on turning it off before she undressed. An orgy, she said, was one thing, but catching double pneumonia in the process was another.

Joanne told about how she had been admitted to the Côte in her pants suit. The producer suggested that the next time she try being admitted without her pants suit. That, he suggested, would be the acid test.

The three of them laughed uproariously. They had been eating and drinking and screwing for several hours and were feeling just great. Cathy rolled the joints herself. The producer spoke admiringly of the color of Cathy's nipples. Cathy spoke admiringly of the size of the producer's wang. He said that when it was fully extended he could place ten silver quar-

ters along its length. Cathy said that they did not make silver
quarters any more. The producer said they did not make wangs
like that any more either. They all laughed immoderately.
Cathy told about the days in California when she made blue
movies. The director suggested that he had always wanted to
direct one. Joanne was enthusiastic but reminded them that
they had no camera. The producer said he carried a mini-
aturized, Japanese-made version of a B.N.C. with a 60-mm
lense concealed in his wang at all times. Joanne said 69-mm.
They all laughed immoderately. Pot on top of a lot of booze
makes the dopiest things seem funny.

So they made the movie.

Then it was light-up time again.

Through the haze Cathy became aware of the pound-
ing on the door.

"Have you ever been picked up by the fuzz?" the
groovy director said.

"No," Cathy said, "but it must hurt a lot."

Everyone laughed immoderately although it was an old
joke. The producer (he had had a picture nominated for an
Academy Award two years before) walked naked to the door
with a joint in his mouth, opened it, and admitted Joanne's
friend, the movie star.

They greeted each other warmly, embracing and ex-
changing darlings and babys. Not faggot darlings and babys.
Hollywood darlings and babys.

"Baby, I knew it *had* to be you," the movie star said to
the producer. "I mean, I knew you were in town and I could
smell the stuff all the way from the Oak Room."

"Nobody busts the Plaza Hotel," the director said.

"Nobody dies on the Dawn Patrol," the movie star
said. He took the joint from the producer's lips and inhaled
deeply, sucking in air at the same time. When he finally ex-
haled, about eight years later, he smiled and joined the group.

He did not recognize Joanne without her pants suit. But he covered nicely. He was, in spite of all his actor crap, a kind man and never, intentionally, hurt anyone's feelings.

The producer told him they had been making movies.

The director suggested they make a second feature.

The movie star said his agents would not let him play in second features.

The producer told him he could have top billing and also get to screw the leading lady.

The movie star said he always screwed his leading ladies.

Cathy said he could also screw the girl who played his leading lady's best friend.

The movie star said well in that case okay.

They all laughed immoderately.

At two o'clock Cathy quietly slipped back into her clothes, selected a clean one-hundred-dollar bill from the wad on the dresser, and tiptoed out of the suite, leaving the producer asleep in a chair. Joanne, the director, and the movie star were laughing and playing in the bathtub.

In the corridor, which did actually *reek* of marijuana, she suddenly remembered that, what with one thing and another, she had never got around to giving Joanne her diaphragm.

Not a plot point, she thought, just an oversight. Without knowing it, she was beginning to think like a best-selling writer.

"Jacqueline Susann did not get where she is today," she said to the sleepy-eyed elevator man, "by having one of her characters forget to give another one of her characters her goddamned diaphragm."

"Jesus," said the sleepy-eyed elevator man.

But without interest or emotion.

2

Getting into the apartment could not have been easier. The latch on the front door was broken, and as Cathy and Joanne between them had lost somewhere in the neighborhood of six hundred and fifty keys in the nine months they had been in residence, they no longer bothered to lock the door of Apartment 4D unless they were at home. As it was Joanne's conviction that the area was teeming with sex maniacs, she had caused a police lock to be installed that would have been adequate to keep the crown jewels in reasonable safety.

But it only worked if someone was inside to work it.

"If neither of us are here," Joanne had said in a blinding flash of logic, "the sex maniacs can screw *themselves,* right?"

Harvey Bernstein was crazed.

He had had his first official drink (as usual) at lunch. He had, of course, been nipping away unofficially since the stab in his instant coffee at nine-thirty-seven that morning. Then he had drunk throughout the afternoon. Then he had read over (a number of times) Cathy's detailed accounts (seven installments by now) of her first few months of kinky sex in the Hollywood Hills. The erotic uses of the electric toothbrush, for instance, were no longer a mystery to him. In fact it all sounded like kind of fun.

At five-thirty-five, filled with passion, resolve, and eighty-six-proof courage, he called his wife with an elaborate story of why he would have to spend the night in New York. He did not reach his wife, which he decided was just as well, as she had absolute pitch, even on the phone, for the number of drinks, official and unofficial, that her husband had consumed during the course of the business day. Instead, he was told by the cleaning woman (Mrs. Edwards) that his wife had been called to the city to deal with some unnamed crisis having to do with their daughter Linda.

As Mrs. Edwards, who should have gone home at four, had been into the bourbon herself, she failed to detect the less-than-faint slur in the speech of the master of the house.

"Sure and it'll do you good," she said heartily. "Every man needs a night out on the town from time to time. Especially if he has to put up day after day with a miserable cunt like your wife, if you'll excuse my language."

It was a barometer of Harvey's condition that he had noticed nothing untoward in Mrs. Edwards' language. They were both, if truth be known, smashed out of their minds.

He did find it interesting that Mrs. Edwards' brogue had become more pronounced in recent months. Particularly since she had been born in Florence, Alabama, and was black as the ace of spades. It came, he imagined, from seeing too many late-night movies on television where all the really high-class help were Irish. Who wanted to be Hattie McDaniel in this day and age?

"Who dat who say who dat when I say who dat?" Harvey said with what seemed to him enormous wit.

"Fuck you, whitey," Mrs. Edwards said.

"Fuck you, too, Mrs. Edwards," Harvey said. "You'll be sure and leave a note for my wife?"

"Certainly, Mr. Bernstein."

"Good night, Mrs. Edwards."

"Good night, Mr. Bernstein."

It seemed to both of them that they had had an amusing, informative, and perfectly plausible conversation.

All this was some time before Harvey had seen Cathy stroking her nipples in the window and had beat it up the street for five ("bar-sized," so they really didn't count as five) martinis.

Alone in the self-service elevator, Harvey felt in many ways like an astronaut. In the first place, he was weightless. In the second, there was a complex array of buttons to push. Up.

Down. G. One, Two, Three, Four, Five, Six. Alarm. He tried to make contact with Mission Control in Houston, but the bastards were all out to lunch or something. He considered pushing Alarm, which is what he felt, but remembering his position as housebreaker, he decided that it might not be wise.

A penciled graffito on the elevator door brought him back to earth with no particular re-entry problem.

"Lillian," someone had written in a semi-literate hand, "takes it up the ass."

Lillian. It reminded him of Gish. Which reminded him of the Old South. Which reminded him of Mrs. Edwards. "Who dat who say who dat when I say who dat?" he said aloud to Mission Control and pushed the button marked Four.

Once on the fourth floor, it was remarkably easy. There were only four apartments; curiously enough, clearly marked A, B, C, and D.

For the hell of it he tried the other three doors first. Knowing that his one and only love was out for the moment, he wondered if perhaps Lillian Of The Elevator might possibly be home. A, B, and C were locked tighter than three chastity belts. D opened to his touch.

There was a card table with a typewriter upon it set up in the middle of the living room. Two of his novels and his two volumes of poetry, in their severe public-library bindings, were on the floor beside the card table. On the table itself was a sheet of yellow paper. He gradually brought his eyes into focus. He saw Cathy's tit-drop. Tears spilled from his eyes. His glasses, like manhole covers, contained the flood. He took them off and shook them over her page, spraying it with tears. He wanted to circle each spot, but he could not find a pencil.

The floor around the card table was littered with rejected pants suits.

It was unspeakably hot in the apartment.

Not bothering to check with Houston, he took the suicide weapon, his beloved P-38, from his hip pocket and craftily hid it beneath a cushion, removed his clothes, and passed out on the couch.

*   *   *   *   *

Cathy tipped the doorman a dollar and asked for the producer's limousine. It was, as she had assumed it would be, standing by. It was, she knew, a matter of principle for personalities in from the Coast to have chauffeur-driven limousines standing by twenty-four hours a day. Larry Harvey, she remembered, had once insisted on a chauffeur-driven Rolls Royce. But things were tighter in Hollywood now. Probably due to all these conglomerate take-overs. Good managers, maybe. But they just didn't understand show business.

She awakened the driver and gave him her address.

As they drove across the 59th Street Bridge, Cathy was feeling groovy. "I'm dappled and drowsy and ready for sleep," she told the driver, who was, she had noticed, very young and really quite good-looking.

The driver apparently could think of no suitable response. That's the difference between chauffeurs and cabdrivers. Chauffeurs keep their yaps shut.

At her front door Cathy reached into her purse and handed the driver Joanne's diaphragm. "Take this up to Suite 1867–8," she said. "It contains the microfilm."

Chapter **THREE**

1

Once inside the door, Cathy briefly considered bolting the police lock. Between the groovy director, the movie star, and now, possibly, the rather good-looking chauffeur who would be arriving presently with her diaphragm, Joanne appeared to be set for the night. On the other hand, if she did decide to come home, it would mean getting up, getting out of bed, and unlocking the door. Which was all right. It was the nightmare of being trapped by a now totally stoned Joanne, who would insist on recounting in appalling detail all the fun and games that she had missed by leaving so early. The lost soap in the tub. What happened when the room-service waiter came to clear away dinner and found them all . . . and on and on and on. In the end Cathy decided to leave the door unlocked. She did not share Joanne's conviction about a prevalence of sex maniacs. In fact, she realized, the only honest-to-God sex maniac she'd ever met in her life was Joanne herself.

This interior dialogue, while tedious to describe, took in actual time something less than a twentieth of a second.

She had closed the door, without locking it, kicked off

her shoes, and begun to unzip her dress (Courrèges) when she
noticed the naked man asleep on the couch. Harvey was, to be
accurate, not completely naked. He was still wearing his eye-
glasses and one sock.

She recognized him immediately as The Man On The
Sidewalk. She studied him for what might or might not have
been a considerable length of time. (Her time-sense perception
was still somewhat distorted by the pot.)

Harvey was a mess. There was no doubt about that.

She reached down and gently plucked his glasses from
his nose. Then she slipped them on herself. The lenses were
about five feet thick but definitely non-telescopic. She took
them off again and placed them out of reach on the card table.
If he did turn out to be a sex maniac, he would obviously be
easier to handle if his vision were slightly impaired.

Gingerly grasping the only non-naked portion of his
body (his left foot), she began to shake him. Presently he
opened his eyes. He blinked several times. "Where am I?" he
said. "Now when I need me," he added. It seemed to Cathy to
be a rather impressive thing for a man in his condition to say.
It had a faintly literary ring that appealed to her.

"You're not by any chance the Astoria Strangler?"
Cathy said.

"What?"

"I mean if you've come here with the idea of raping,
strangling, and murdering anybody, you can just put it right
out of your mind. Dismiss the entire notion. Immediately."

"I love you," Harvey said.

Then he closed his eyes again and appeared to drift off
into sleep once more.

There followed a series of "if only's."

If only she had had the sense not to go to the Plaza and
to lock the door after Joanne had gone.

If only she had had the sense to remain at the

Plaza, laughing, splashing, and frolicking with the others in the air-conditioned bathroom.

If only she had had the sense to ask the good-looking chauffeur up for a drink. Together they could have got the body on the couch into its clothes, down the stairs, into the limousine, and out of her life.

If only . . .

She seemed to have run out of them.

Halfheartedly she shook his foot once more. Then she stopped. Actually there was no point in awakening him until she figured out what she was going to do with him once he was awake.

It was stifling in the apartment.

Sweat caused Harvey's body to glisten. It was rather hairy in an unattractive way, which made him seem even more pathetic. There were tiny tufts of damp fur on each of his shoulders. Cathy found them curiously touching.

She wondered who he had thought he was talking to when he said, "I love you."

It was a phrase that she had not heard from a man's lips in years. I want you—yes. You have a beautiful behind— yes. I'll give you a thousand dollars to go to Vegas with me for the weekend—yes. But, I love you—not in a very long time.

Jigger was the last, she guessed. And he *had* loved her, in his fashion. At least he had actually said the words. It was the sentence that had immediately followed his declaration that had dimmed its romantic flavor just a little. "Listen," Jigger had said, "Gersten says he'll give us five hundred apiece to make a stag reel for him."

It was like an old Dan Dailey–Betty Grable musical. She knew damn well Gersten didn't want the team, honey, he just wanted her. But she didn't have the heart to break it to Jigger. His ego was in a very delicate condition at that time anyway. The faggot who had been keeping him had cut him off with nothing but the Thunderbird, and any further rejection might have been just enough to send him off the deep end.

So she and Jigger had made the film. In a motel on Ventura Boulevard. Once in front of a camera, Jigger had suddenly turned ham. He had continuously hogged the key light. He had also insisted on the final close-up. A tight shot of his face as he simulated orgasm. They'd asked her to squat down under the camera and out of the picture and give him a helping hand, but she'd said screw that, it's his close-up, let him come any way he can. Then, for a topper, Gersten insisted he'd meant five hundred for the team. Not apiece.

So much for I love you.

Cathy had a sudden impulse to cover Harvey with a blanket, tuck him in tenderly, kiss him on the brow, and let him sleep it off. But as the temperature in the apartment was at least ninety degrees, covering him with a blanket would not have been the act of kindness that it might have been on a different occasion.

Instead, Cathy went into her bedroom and carefully took off and hung up the Courrèges. Then, really without thinking about it, she stepped into the shower. The cool water was both soothing and refreshing. It seemed to wash away the last of the pot. It was only as she was beginning to relax that she remembered the movie *Psycho*. The stabbing-in-the-shower scene came to mind with remarkable vividness. Maybe the sad, wet, hairy thing on her couch *was* a sex maniac. Maybe he was only pretending to be asleep. Maybe at this very moment he, now fully alert, 20/20 vision restored by the easily found glasses, was rummaging wildly around the kitchen in search of the bread knife.

Without bothering to turn off the water, she dashed out of the shower, blindly grabbing for a towel as she went. In the living room his glasses were still on the card table. His clothes were still on the floor (mingled, as they had been, with

Joanne's pants suits). But the front door was now open and he was gone.

Holding the towel in front of her (in her haste she had taken a small face towel, not a large bath towel), she went to the door and peered down the corridor. Harvey, naked except for his left sock (black), was lurching toward the elevator, ringing bells at each of the other three apartments as he went.

"Now you come back here!" Cathy shouted after him. "I'm really vexed with you!"

Vexed? She had not heard or used that word since she left Webb City God knows how many years ago. It had been one of Grandpa's favorites, though.

Harvey disappeared into the elevator and the doors closed behind him.

If there had ever been a moment to use the police lock, this was it.

"Jesus-fucking-shit-ass-Christ!" Cathy said aloud as she strode down the corridor toward the elevator, not even bothering to hold the towel up in front of her. Two of the other apartments on the floor were occupied by hookers and the third by a pair of really very sweet faggots who loved to cook and occasionally asked Cathy and Joanne in for Sunday brunch. Bloody Marys, baked ham, and wonderful homemade bread.

"You know what you are?" Cathy said aloud as she jammed her thumb against the elevator button and held it there. "You are that greatest of all literary clichés"—she was quoting verbatim from one of her instructor HB's critiques— "the prostitute with a heart of gold.

"And what a dumb fucking thing *that* is to be," she added as somewhere deep in the intestines of the building the elevator rumbled, farted, and changed direction.

When the elevator doors opened, Harvey was seated on the floor in a corner, crying.

"Now really," Cathy said, "I am *terribly* vexed with you!"

Harvey tried, manfully, to rise. He sank back, however, almost at once. She entered the elevator and attempted to pull him to his feet. The elevator doors closed behind her.

Someone, somewhere in the building, had pushed a button.

In her mind Cathy rapidly improvised a series of possible costumes that would adequately cover both of them, giving, in addition, perhaps, the illusion of Fun City Summer Chic. Two of the Beautiful People returning from a costume ball at Gloria Vanderbilt Cooper's, for example. Since she had little to work with but one black sock and one wet face towel, it did not seem promising.

Cathy draped the towel over Harvey's lap.

The elevator doors opened.

The couple in the lobby stood there beaming foolishly. She was a professional acquaintance who lived in 3D. He was wearing a white dinner jacket. One of her false eyelashes had come loose and was dangling precariously. Harvey moaned.

"Twenty-two dollars, please," Cathy said without hesitation. "Unless, of course, you already have the tickets."

The gentleman in the white dinner jacket reached automatically for his wallet. Gentlemen in white dinner jackets always reach automatically for their wallets. This was one of the few observable absolutes in Cathy's life.

"This is the Elevator Theater," Cathy said, "the smallest, dirtiest, most uncomfortable, most expensive Off-off-off Broadway entertainment in town."

"Remember, darling," White Dinner Jacket's companion said, instantly picking up the cue, "we tried to get tickets from the captain at '21,' but he said there was no chance at any price?"

"Suicide to Mission Control," Harvey said, lying now

on the floor, the towel for some reason over his face. "Mission Control, this is Suicide. Do you read me? Over and out."

"Grand," White Dinner Jacket said. "I only come to New York once a year. I like to catch as many shows as I can."

He took a fifty-dollar bill from his wallet and handed it to Cathy. "Keep the change," he said.

Cathy handed the fifty to the girl. The girl pushed Three. The elevator doors closed.

"Profusely illustrated souvenir programs are on sale inside," Cathy said to keep the ball rolling till the elevator reached the third floor. On the third floor White Dinner Jacket made a friendly but ineffective grab at Cathy's left breast. His companion slapped his wrist. "Naughty, naughty!" she said. "You don't want to leave it all in the gym."

Harvey moaned something incomprehensible through his towel.

The elevator doors opened and eventually closed behind them.

Cathy pushed Four.

"You are a disgrace," Cathy said to Harvey. "A public disgrace."

"I love you," Harvey said and attempted, unsuccessfully, to pass out again.

2

As the late Humphrey Bogart once said, "At four o'clock in the morning you got to figure everybody's drunk."

It was and is a sound observation.

God knows, Harvey was drunk. And the couple now safely landed on the third floor was certainly drunk. By this time, however, Cathy was off her maryjane high and was beginning to feel ever so slightly depressed.

She had hauled Harvey out of the elevator, down the corridor, and back into the apartment.

The telephone was ringing.

It was Joanne. The chauffeur was on the bedroom extension. The party was just getting good. Why didn't Cathy come on back in. And bring their piggy bank. The chauffeur's had proved to be equal to if not larger than the producer's. Eleven silver quarters were urgently needed for a test match. But they had run out of change. And the cashier's desk was closed for the night. They were all also pretty hungry and could Cathy just stop at Reuben's on the way in and pick up . . . she was still getting the orders organized, which kinds of sandwiches on what kinds of bread, some with mustard and some without, when Cathy hung up the phone.

Like Cathy, Harvey Bernstein had suddenly become more alert.

"You do not have, by any chance, something to drink on the premises? If not, and I wish to put you to no inconvenience, I am sure there is an all-nite . . . it is curious that the word night is frequently spelled N I T E at establishments which are open all—an unforgivable corruption . . . liquor store open somewhere in the neighborhood. I think frozen daiquiris would be nice. If you have a fresh lime or two, I shall go out and get the rum." He started for the door.

Cathy, seizing him by his shoulder tufts, pushed him back onto the couch.

"For God's sake, put on your glasses," Cathy said.

He did so.

"And either get dressed or take off that one sock. You look ridiculous."

Obediently Harvey removed his sock.

He observed her carefully through his glasses for a moment or two, then rose and moved toward the telephone, careening off the furniture as he went.

Cathy stopped him just in time.

"Who do you want to call?"

"Whom do I want to call. Not *who* do I want to call. I want to call Max Wilk, Ed Hotchner, and Max Shulman and beg their forgiveness. You *are* real!"

"My God," Cathy said. "You're Harvey-fucking-*Bernstein!*"

3

Harvey Bernstein burst into tears.

"I have been in love with but three women in my forty-six years of life," he said between sobs. "And you are the only one of them I have been privileged to meet in person."

Cathy said nothing. There seemed to be little to say.

Harvey found a pair of trousers on the floor, picked them up, and attempted to put them on. They were Joanne's and he could not get them over his kneecaps. Cathy knelt down and helped him disentangle himself, lifting first one of his feet and then the other.

"I cried myself to sleep the night my first love, Alice Faye, married Phil Harris," he continued, reaching into a nonexistent pocket for a nonexistent handkerchief. He finally settled the problem by removing his glasses and wiping his eyes with the back of his hand.

"I have, over the years, published a series of critical essays attacking Arthur Miller in such periodicals as the *Diners' Club Magazine*. Not because I did not admire his work but because of my second love, Marilyn. You, Cathy Lewis Lovibond Lombard Lamont," he added, "are all that is left to me now. Cathy, I love you!"

He was sweaty and naked and drunk, and his nose was running. He had lost his glasses again. He was covered with hair in all the wrong places. He was just awful. But he loved her. He did not say he wanted her. He did not say she had a beautiful behind. He did not offer her a thousand dollars to go to Vegas with him for the weekend. He said: *I love you.*

Tears welled up in Cathy's eyes.

"Darling," Cathy said. "What can I do? Just tell me what I can do."

"I love you," Harvey said. He stood, swaying gently, by the couch.

Cathy was still kneeling in front of him, holding the trousers of Joanne's pants suit in her hand. They were plum-colored, slashed deeply at the sides, and vaguely held together by what seemed to be white shoelaces. Martin must have been really desperate, letting her into the Côte in *that* getup.

"I love you," Harvey said.

Cathy tried. But at that moment and in his condition it turned out not to be an intensely practical proposition.

"Later, darling," Cathy said. "I promise! I promise!"

"I love you," Harvey said.

She got up, took him by the hand, and led him to the bathroom. The shower, naturally, was still running.

Gracefully leading the way, she escorted him under it. Somehow, en route, he had found his glasses again and put them on. This caused a minor problem under the cold cascading water. She took them off his nose and placed them carefully in the soap dish, removing the soap.

For a while they stood together without touching. Then she opened her arms to him. He moved toward her, slipped on the soap, bounched off the tile wall, and landed on his head.

Cathy managed to get his inert body out of the shower before he actually drowned.

Chapter FOUR

1

Harvey Bernstein's first thought when consciousness finally returned was that he had gone blind. As far as he could tell, his eyes were open. He fluttered the lids a few times experimentally, but the view remained the same. Total blackness.

For a moment or two the idea of blindness did seem to have its brighter side. He would not have to read the conclusion of Mrs. Edna Mortimer (housewife)'s novel or the further non-adventures of Harrison Bradley, probably the world's dullest and most illiterate general since the late Dwight D. Eisenhower. Charles Douglas Potter's Albert's bulging crotch would be out of his life forever. People would be kind to him. Old ladies would help him across streets. He could spend his days listening to recordings of Orson Welles reading from the Bible. He wondered if his Major Medical covered loss of sight.

Tentatively he raised his head a few inches from what seemed to be a pillow. A crack of light coming from under a door crossed his line of vision. For a moment he felt almost wistful. So he was not blind, after all. He was just lying in a strange room with blackout curtains drawn. He had a bone-crushing hangover. Certain highlights of the preceding twenty-four hours slowly returned to him.

He began to tremble.

Icy sweat broke out, drenching his entire body.

Then he remembered Cathy leading him gently to the shower, and tears filled his eyes. He had been crying and sweating almost incessantly for the past two days. All in all he must have exuded several gallons of fluid. Of course he had replaced at least that much by his intake of neutral grain spirits.

Beside him in the bed, someone stirred.

Cathy! Cathy! Cathy!

Experimentally, he reached out an exploring hand. What it encountered was a breast.

She stirred a little but did not waken.

Suddenly he was no longer trembling, crying, or sweat-ign. As he tenderly caressed her sleeping body, the panic drained from him. She moaned a little happy moan as her nipples stiffened to his touch. Gently she took his hand and guided it downward between her legs. Then she herself reached downward.

When someone is especially skilled and practiced at a given action, it is often colloquially said that he or she can do it in his sleep.

No word was spoken as, in her sleep, she deftly moved him into herself. It was mad, trancelike, and extremely pleas-ant. They came together, and at the ultimate moment Harvey, not wanting to break the dream, refrained from whispering "Ointment" into her ear. Contented, she guided him out of herself, rolled onto her side, and moved happily off into deeper sleep.

Harvey rose from the bed and, on tiptoe, trying in equal parts not to awaken her and also not to trip over some-thing and break his neck, groped his way toward the crack of light under the door. He finally made it.

In the living room he *was* temporarily blinded by the blazing afternoon sunlight. He staggered to the kitchen.

"Good morning, darling," Cathy said. She was seated naked at the table, studying the *Wall Street Journal,* a cup of coffee in her hand. "I was beginning to wonder if you were still alive."

Harvey Bernstein did the only sensible thing a man could do at such a moment. He turned and ran into the bathroom, locking the door behind him.

2

Any American male who has survived for forty-six years has, at least once, experienced the sensation of knowing that he is at that moment stark raving mad but still sane enough to be aware of the fact.

With the sane part of his mind he watched his insane self calmly shower, shave (there was a razor in the medicine cabinet but no shaving cream; he simply lathered his face with a cake of Yardley's soap), comb his hair, wrap a bath towel around his waist, and return to the living room. Cathy, still naked, was stretched out on the couch reading a copy of *U.S. News and World Report.*

His sane self heard the insane part say, "Do you mind if I use the telephone? I think I'd better call my wife."

3

Margery and Max had returned from the motel at eleven-thirty the night before. They were prepared for the confrontation scene with Harvey. Mrs. Edwards had finished the bourbon and left the house, forgetting entirely Harvey's request that she leave a note. Harvey was not there. They had waited until two o'clock. Finally Max had said, "Why don't we just leave him a note, pack your stuff, and get out of here. The wedding's at eleven and our plane's at two. If we leave pretty soon, we can drive to town and get some sleep."

Margery was disappointed. She had been spoiling for a really good confrontation scene for twenty-two years.

"I wouldn't know how to tell him in a note."

"Let's divide the labor. I'm the writer, you're the housewife. You pack and I'll write the note. Does the silly bastard have a typewriter around here someplace?"

"You are a very beautiful man," Margery had said. "I think there's an Olivetti portable in the hall closet."

4

"What will you tell her?" Cathy asked as the Insane Harvey dialed the number.

"I shall tell her that I was called to New York to meet with a publisher who wishes to reprint my three novels and two volumes of poetry in paperback. I will tell her that we wined and dined, not wisely but too well, at Pavillon and then repaired to the Oak Room Bar, and when that at last closed, moved on to an after-hours bottle club of which he is an old and valued member. I will explain that it was all a matter of business."

The Sane Harvey listened to this nonsense, aghast.

At the other end the phone was ringing.

Presently Mrs. Edwards picked up the receiver. She had arrived at work with a hangover down to her toenails. But glass in hand, she was making a nice recovery.

"Top o' the morning to you, Mr. Bernstein," Mrs. Edwards said.

"How are you, Mrs. Edwards?" Harvey asked.

"The better for hearing the sound of your voice, lad," Mrs. Edwards said between sips.

"Listen, Mrs. Edwards, will you please knock off the Gallic charm and put Mrs. Bernstein on the phone!"

"Fuck you, whitey," Mrs. Edwards said.

"Fuck you, Mrs. Edwards," Harvey said. "Would you please get Mrs. Bernstein?"

Mrs. Edwards, reduced by drink to an uncommonly low threshold of sentimentality, burst into tears.

"Missus Bernstein done gone," Mrs. Edwards said. "She done gone and run off with that no-count white trash Max Wilk. She done left bag and baggage. She done left you a note."

"Who dat?" Harvey said.

"Who dat who say who dat?" Mrs. Edwards said.

"Who dat who say who dat when I say who dat?" the Insane Harvey said.

Cathy, who could hear only one end of it, thought it was the most mysterious and in some ways most glorious conversation she had ever listened to.

"Mrs. Bernstein done gone off with Max *Wilk?*" Harvey asked.

"Sure and she is after leaving me a note and also one for yourself. In my note she says for me to give you your note 'if and when that drunken son of a bitch shows up.' Her very words, Mr. Bernstein. On my children's heads."

"You are, Mrs. Edwards, to the best of my knowledge, childless," Harvey said.

" 'Tis the good Lord's will," said Mrs. Edwards. "But it sure ain't for lack of trying."

"Would you be good enough, Mrs. Edwards, to open Mrs. Bernstein's note to me and read it aloud over the phone."

"Of course, Mr. Bernstein. Just let me freshen my drink."

"What in God's name is going on?" Cathy asked.

"Apparently my wife Margery has run off with a best-selling writer named Max Wilk. She has left me a note. Mrs. Edwards, our cleaning woman, will read it to me. As soon as she freshens her drink."

"Would you like some coffee?" Cathy said.

"I would like a drink," Harvey said. The sane and insane were beginning to merge. Harvey was fighting his way back to what, in his case, passed for normalcy.

"Very sound," Cathy said. She went to the kitchen and fixed two vodka and Frescas.

Mrs. Edwards returned to the phone.

"No goddamned cigarettes in the house," Mrs. Edwards said. "But I found some of Miss Linda's pot. She keeps a stash in an envelope in the Family Bible. II Samuel 19. There's a nice little bit right here. '*And Shimel the son of Gera, a Benjamite, which was of Bahurim, hasted and came down with the men of Judah to meet king David.*' You wouldn't know, would you, where she keeps the cigarette papers?"

"Will you please just read me the note."

"Certainly."

*   *   *   *   *

"Dear Harvey,

It is now two o'clock in the morning. Margery is upstairs packing. I am truly sorry to tell you this, but Margery and I have been in love since we worked together on the Westport unwed mothers thing; a project in which you, callous to the plight of numberless unfortunate young girls, evinced no interest whatever. Indeed, as I recall, even declaring, drunkenly one evening, that you were in favor of unwed mothers. In any case we have been conducting an affair for the last two months. We are leaving for Europe tomorrow afternoon. (George V, Paris, for a week. And from the 17th on, the Gritti, Venice—should you for any reason wish to communicate.) My new novel has been accepted by the Book-of-the-Month Club. Phil Roth will review it in the *New York Review of Books*. I've seen the galleys, of which he was kind enough to send me an advance copy. Sensational! But I digress. Margery asked me to tell you that your daughter Linda and her fiancé Lester are to be married at eleven tomorrow at the Abyssinian Baptist Church by the Reverend Adam Clayton Powell himself. If you sober up sufficiently, you are most certainly invited to attend. (Perhaps it is important inter-racial efforts such as this one that had in the past caused the Reverend Mr. Powell to be so often absent from Washington. Only history will tell us if his was not in the end the wiser course.) In the matter of Linda, I congratulate you. You have not failed her. In the matter of Margery, I express regrets. You are failed. I am successful. You drink. I no longer do so. (Gout.) Do whatever you see fit in the matter of a divorce. Your children are grown. Margery is liberated. We are in no haste to marry so you can take your time and think it over.

Margery asks me to add (she has just come down with the suitcases) that she is writing a five-thousand-dollar check on your joint account at City National as a wedding present to your daughter. The house is yours. You have your job. You should be, she feels, okay. She wants, of course, no alimony. As a gesture of good will I shall undertake to finance Bruce through Berkeley. He is a beautiful boy and I can see no reason for your frequent and clearly uncalled-for remarks about his appearance. Personally I am proud to have a semi-stepson with the moral fiber to take the action he did against the Dean of Admissions. I shall also be proud to handle the bail money. Good-bye for now. And good luck. Believe me, Harve, old buddy, I'll take good care of her.

Fondly,

Max

P.S. I hear you're reviewing my new book for the *Diners' Club Magazine.* I hope you like it. I think it's the most important thing I've done so far. Phil thinks so too, apparently."

5 3

*   *   *   *   *

"Mrs. Edwards," Harvey said, "listen to me carefully. I want you to go to my desk in the study and in the top drawer you will find my checkbook. I want you to get it and bring it back to the phone with you."

Mrs. Edwards, who was seated with her feet propped up on Harvey's desk, put down her glass, opened the drawer, and took out the checkbook.

"Done and done, me bucko."

"All right now. Turn to the page with the last balance on it and tell me what the figure is."

"Before the check for five big ones for Miss Linda," Mrs. Edwards said after a moment, "you had five thousand one hundred and eighty dollars and seventy-two cents. Now you got one hundred and eighty dollars and seventy-two cents."

"My God."

"By the by," Mrs. Edwards said. "You owe me for two days this week and two days last week. That's eighty dollars."

"I'll send you a check."

"Your credit is good with me any time," Mrs. Edwards said, making a face. She disliked vodka but had unfortunately finished the bourbon yesterday. "I don't suppose you'll be after wanting me to come in tomorrow?"

"I don't think I can afford you."

There was a pause.

"Well, have a nice day, Mr. Bernstein."

"You too, Mrs. Edwards."

Harvey slowly hung up the phone.

"My God," Cathy said. "What was *that* all about?"

He told her.

In detail.

About halfway through she began to giggle. By the end she was laughing so hard that tears were rolling down her cheeks. She undid the towel he was wearing around his waist and used it to wipe her eyes.

Then she kissed him. Gently at first. Then harder. After a while she whispered, "Come on, darling, let's go to bed."

Then Harvey remembered.

"I . . . I . . . can't," he said.

"Why not, darling?"

"I've just *been* to bed."

"I mean to make love."

"I just *made* love. A few minutes ago. With someone in there. It was dark. I thought it was you."

Then Cathy started to laugh again.

"How was it?" she asked through her giggles.

"Very nice, I guess," Harvey said. "Except she never really woke up."

"Joanne's good, darling. But I'm better. You'll see."

"I'm forty-six years old," Harvey said. "I want to. Oh, God, how I want to. But I don't think I can."

"Let that be my problem. I know the magic words."

She said them and meant them.

"I love you."

They never made it to the bedroom. The kitchen floor was just fine.

$*$ $*$ $*$ $*$ $*$

"Ointment!"

$*$ $*$ $*$ $*$ $*$

"Ointment!"

$*$ $*$ $*$ $*$ $*$

"Ointment!"

$*$ $*$ $*$ $*$ $*$

For a man who was, indeed, forty-six and who had in his time consumed the equivalent of three railroad tank cars full of alcohol it really was an extraordinary performance.

But then Cathy was an extraordinary girl.

After the second one he had said, "My God, it's not possible. I'm an old *man*."

"That's right, darling," Cathy had said, "you're the Warren Beatty of Senior City."

That had turned him on for the third one. That and a couple of little things that Cathy herself hadn't even known she knew. Love, not necessity, is often the mother of invention.

5

They were lying tangled in each other's arms, asleep on the floor when, sometime later, Joanne, still drunk, stoned and screwed silly, wandered into the kitchen, thinking it was the bathroom, in search of an Alka-Seltzer.

One glance was enough for her to know that her deepest fears had finally been realized. She instantly dashed to the phone in the living room and dialled 911, the emergency number.

"Police!" she said. "A sex maniac has broken into our apartment and raped my roommate!"

Then she gave the address and apartment number.

Then, realizing that there was probably more than one sex maniac running around loose in the Borough of Queens, she carefully fastened the police lock.

Sensing with pride that she had done something both resourceful and possibly even heroic (she could no longer remember what it was), she drifted back to her bedroom and was sleeping peacefully long before the emergency squad arrived forty minutes later.

Chapter FIVE

1

About ten minutes after Joanne's phone call, Cathy and Harvey awoke simultaneously. They both felt marvelous. And they were both starving.

"Steak," Cathy said.

"Very rare," Harvey said.

"Blood rare," Cathy said. "Warm on the inside it must be. But just barely."

"Charred, however, on the outside."

"Exactly. With thick slices of tomato and raw onion, lightly garnished with a happy mixture of imported olive oil, red wine vinegar, and a dash of English mustard. Salt and freshly ground black pepper, to taste."

They were under the shower again, passing the soap back and forth, caressing each other with warm suds.

"Golden-brown French fries with plenty of catsup to glunk them in," Cathy said.

"Or maybe baked with sour cream and chives," Harvey said.

"Or you know what's great?" Cathy said, gently soap-

ing his far-more-vital-than-he-had-ever-imagined-it-could-be
organ. "We could have them scoop out baked potatoes and put
the skins back in a hot oven for a couple of minutes and then
eat them with our fingers all glopped in butter."

In real life, if not in literature, the conversation after
three really sensational screws (four in Harvey's case) generally
turns into a sensually detailed discussion of food.

Cathy's face, framed as it was by her plastic shower
cap and devoid of makeup, did not look in the least childlike
and innocent. It looked depraved, lascivious, and totally
wanton. Which is exactly how it should have looked.

They dried each other.

They organized their hair.

Cathy put on slacks and a shirt.

Harvey put on yesterday's clothes. Then he remembered
the gun.

"You'd better keep this," Harvey said. "I was planning
to commit suicide."

Cathy put the gun in her oversize handbag.

"I don't think that will be necessary," she said.

"Neither do I."

"I love you."

"I love you."

Cathy unfastened the police lock and closed the door
behind them.

They took a cab to a place in Brooklyn called Peter
Luger's, where they understand about steak blood rare but still
warm on the inside. They also know about hot, crisp baked
potato skins and plenty of butter. The draught beer is served
in huge beady-cold glass steins.

The martinis are automatically served double in chilled
wine glasses. The lemon peels are sliced paper-thin and throw
a fine spray of oil over the surface when properly twisted.

All of which tends to keep things going till the steaks arrive.

The white linen cloths are long enough so you can mingle legs under the table.

"Enjoy your dinner," the waiter said.

They did.

2

Officers Bertolotti and Steinkamp burst through the unlocked door of Apartment 4D with guns drawn. It had been a quiet afternoon. Hot and boring. Finally they had parked their vehicle at the shady end of a deserted alley. Bertolotti had fallen asleep immediately. Steinkamp found that the incessant crackling of the radio interfered with his study of a printed symposium in the current *Playboy*. The Reverend Charles Gardiner of All Saints Church, St. Albans, seemed to feel that masturbation was okay if conducted in private between consenting adult. This was a new thought for Steinkamp. He shut off the annoying radio the better to digest it. Later he too fell asleep, wondering what had become of Jo Collins, Playmate of the Year in 1965.

Eventually Bertolotti had awakened and, after enjoying the silence for a while, switched the radio back on in time to pick up the third call for the rape at 42931 Northern Boulevard.

There were, naturally, pants suits scattered all over the living-room floor.

"My God!" Bertolotti said.

"Don't touch anything," Steinkamp said. He had six months' seniority on Bertolotti and was therefore technically in charge.

They were twenty-three and twenty-four respectively and had both joined the police force in the hope of beating the draft.

"If this thing is big enough," Steinkamp said, "I mean like if it's murder and rape *and* there's drugs involved, maybe we'll both make sergeant."

"They don't draft sergeants, do they?" Bertolotti said.

"God, I hope not," Steinkamp said just before he sneezed, accidentally discharging his revolver through the closed bathroom door, the bullet lodging in the tiled wall.

"Jesus! Watch yourself!" Bertolotti said.

"Just trying to flush the bastard out," Steinkamp said, with no particular conviction.

At the sound of the shot Joanne leaped from her bed and staggered into the living room. The light was blinding.

"You're safe now, ma'am," Steinkamp said. "We're here!"

Bertolotti's jaw dropped. He had always been a tit man.

"We are police officers," Steinkamp said. "Emergency squad."

Joanne yawned.

The last thing she could remember with any clarity was being in the bathtub with the movie star and the groovy director.

"Listen," Joanne said. "Why don't you mad characters fix yourself a drink? I'll roll us all another joint."

Steinkamp and Bertolotti looked at each other. Then they looked at Joanne.

"What about the rapist?" Steinkamp said.

Oddly enough, "The Rapist" had been the title they had given to the imaginary movie they had made back at the hotel suite. The second one. The one with the movie star.

"Cut and print," Joanne said. "Unless maybe you think we need some retakes."

The younger one, Bertolotti, was kind of groovy-looking. Joanne decided to fix the drinks herself.

"Vodka and Fresca?"

There was a long pause.

Bertolotti looked at Steinkamp.

"Well, maybe just one," Steinkamp said, "while we interrogate the witness."

"Maybe we ought to lock the door," Bertolotti said.

"It's a police lock," Joanne said.

"What the hell," Steinkamp said. "We're the police."

They all laughed immoderately.

They divided the labor. Steinkamp locked the door. Bertolotti fixed the drinks. Joanne rolled the joints.

It was terribly hot in the apartment.

After a while Joanne suggested to her guests that they take off their clothes.

"Absolutely right," Steinkamp said, loosening his tie. "Do nothing to disgrace the uniform."

They all laughed immoderately.

* * * * *

On the street below, the radio in the abandoned police car continued to crackle.

* * * * *

Ominously.

3

When the cab turned the corner, there were five squad cars and a paddy wagon parked in front of the building.

"Gracious," Cathy said.

They stopped the cab and got out across the street. They joined the crowd and watched as Bertolotti, his shirttail out, Steinkamp, his hands above his head, and Joanne, wearing the bottom half of a pants suit and a policeman's cap, were hustled into the wagon. They were followed by the two nice faggots who lived in 4C (they had been cooking dinner when the cops broke in and had come out into the corridor to see what was going on; the *filet de boeuf* Wellington was still in the oven. The crust would be burnt to a crisp) and the Man in the White Dinner Jacket who had been going down in the elevator. The Man in the White Dinner Jacket was reaching automatically for his wallet as the barred door closed behind him.

"Darling," Cathy said. "I think it's time we were moving on."

They got back into the cab.

"Kennedy Airport," Cathy said to the driver.

"Where are we going?" Harvey could feel the feeling of being insane and knowing it starting to creep over him again.

"The Coast, I think," Cathy said.

"But how can I?" the Sane Harvey said. "I have my job."

"You hate your job."

"What about my house?"

"Wire a real-estate man and tell him to sell it."

"How will we live?"

"You'll teach me to be a best-selling writer."

"I am forty-six years old. I have responsibilities."

"To who?"

"To *whom*," Harvey said automatically.

"To whom?"

Harvey thought a minute.

Max was taking care of Margery and Bruce. He, himself, had apparently taken care of Linda and Lester.

"Mrs. Mortimer, the General, and Charles Douglas Potter," was the best he could come up with.

"Whom are they?"

"*Who* are they."

"I'll never get it straight."

"Of course you will. Who is the subject. Whom is the object. They are my students."

"I can't bear the thought of you teaching anyone but me. Promise you'll never explain the difference between who and whom to anyone else as long as we're together. I would consider it an act of infidelity."

"How about the difference between further and farther?" the Insane Harvey said. "You've never been able to get that straight either."

"What about the correct usage of that and which?" Cathy said. She knew she had him there. In one of his more drunken letters he had explained that only a man named Fowler and a man named Harold Ross who had been editor of *The New Yorker* magazine *really* understood the difference between that and which, and since they were both dead he didn't think it actually mattered.

His inability to understand the basic usage of that and which had always haunted him. He had once asked Max Wilk and Max hadn't known either. Oh, he'd bull-shitted a little, but in the end he really didn't know. It was like knowing how they figure what day Easter is going to be each year. Everyone *thinks* he knows but he doesn't. Think about it sometime. Not now. But sometime.

"I have no toothbrush," the Insane Harvey said, changing the subject.

"They have toothbrushes in California," Cathy said. "They also have them in the can on the plane. With itty-bitty tubes of toothpaste. I will steal you half a dozen. They also have itty-bitty combs and itty-bitty Wash'n Dri's and itty-bitty samples of after-shave lotion and itty-bitty bottles of men's cologne. I favor Russian Leather myself."

"I also have no money," the Sane Harvey said.

"Which reminds me," Cathy said.

She tapped the driver on the shoulder. "Would you

please stop at the YWCA on Lefferts Boulevard," she said. "I have to pick up something."

The something she picked up (from her locker—she was a member and used the pool faithfully three times a week) was not her tank suit, not her extra hairbrush, and not a spray tin of something called Right Guard that she had been talked into buying from the locker-room lady who looked as if she were saving up for a trip to Denmark for a reverse Christine Jorgensen operation and which Cathy had never used, figuring correctly that people smell better than stuff that is sprayed out of cans. What she did pick up was a Pan Am bag that contained two hundred and forty-five one-hundred-dollar bills.

There had been two hundred and fifty of them, but she had dipped into capital for the first time in three years in order to become a Best-Selling Writer.

"It's always more expensive when you're traveling," she explained to Harvey as the cab turned off Lefferts toward the Van Wyck Expressway and the airport, "but if we don't go absolutely *bonkers*"—in spite of Joanne she rather liked the word—"I think we should be able to live very nicely on, say, five hundred a week. That gives us almost a year. Besides," she added thoughtfully, "if we ever want to splurge a little, I can always get a job with Gersten."

"*Making dirty movies?*"

Cathy shook her head. "*Writing* them. If you can teach me to be a best-selling writer, you can certainly teach me how to write dirty movies!"

"The last movie I saw was *Alexander's Ragtime Band* with Tyrone Power, Don Ameche, and Alice Faye. I could never bring myself to see a film of Marilyn's. The sight of those ravishing lips, seventy feet wide on the giant screen, would have been more than I could bear."

Cathy patted his hand and hoped that he would not begin to cry again.

He didn't.

Instead, he began to sing in a deep emotion-filled baritone "These Foolish Things," a song from his youth.

Aesthetically it would have been better if he *had* cried, as he was tone-deaf and could not carry a tune.

* * * * *

The last Royal Ambassador Flight nonstop to LA was at ten o'clock, boarding at nine-forty-five.

"Family Plan," Cathy said to the passenger agent as she counted out hundred-dollar bills. "I am joining my husband on a business trip to California. He designs aerospace ground-to-air missile systems for Lockheed. He was a test pilot before they grounded him and stuck him behind a desk. That was after the last crash. Engine failure at twelve hundred miles an hour. But he walked away from it."

"I volunteered for the original astronaut program," the Insane Harvey said. "But I was turned down because of my religion."

The passenger agent, whose name, according to the plastic tag he wore on his breast pocket, was Berkowitz, winked.

"You got *nachas*," he whispered. "Let the goyim go to the moon. It's probably restricted anyway."

He scribbled something on a small, engraved card. "Here," he said, resuming his normal, homey TWA voice. "Why don't you folks wait up in the Ambassador Club. I think you'll find it's more comfortable."

On the way upstairs Cathy stopped at the newsstand and bought a number of paperbacks. The ones with the sexiest covers.

"Homework," she said.

Inside the Ambassador Club they sat in the lounge, holding hands and sipping brandy until it was time to board.

Chapter **S I X**

1

Tracy Steele was (quite literally) scared shitless of flying. That was why he always took the night flight to the Coast. He felt safer, somehow, if it was dark out and he couldn't see the ground. He was also frightened of being alone. That's why he had it in his contract that Tiger Wilson, his stunt double, bodyguard, trainer, chauffeur (Tracy was also terrified of driving), procurer, social secretary, and nominal vice-president of several of his less important corporations (the one that owned the restaurants which he occasionally found it necessary to buy, for example), was available to him twenty-four hours a day, seven days a week, three hundred and sixty-five days a year. Tiger's official title, as far as the studio was concerned, was dialogue director. That way he could be paid a grand a week plus expenses and still be written off against whatever picture Tracy was either making or preparing at the moment.

At the moment Tracy was seated, pants down, in a booth in the gentlemen's room, located behind the bar, through the cloakroom, in the Ambassador Club.

Tiger, a double vodka stinger in his hand, knocked on the door. "You okay, Trace?"

Tracy Steele groaned.

"Pass it under the door, will you, baby?"

Tiger passed the stinger under the door.

"Thanks, sweetheart," Tracy said.

Vodka stingers helped settle Trace's stomach before a flight.

"Take it easy," Tiger said. "In six hours we'll be back in Beverly Hills."

"What's the movie?" Tracy said.

Tiger told him.

"Shit," Trace said. It was one of his own pictures. "You should have checked it out." Unlike most actors, the sight of himself on the screen caused him to throw up uncontrollably.

"I got it all organized," Tiger said. "They put us on board first. We sit up in the lounge, play gin, and horse around with the stewardesses."

Somewhat mollified, Trace said, "Anybody else on the plane?"

"Nope," Tiger said. "I checked the manifest."

It was a well-known fact that Tracy Steele refused to fly at all if there was someone more important than himself on the plane. It was a matter of who got top billing in case of a crash. "Tracy Steele and Sixty-seven Killed in Air Disaster" was one thing. But being one of the sixty-seven was another. A lifelong Republican, he had once leaped off a plane when the senior Senator from New York had, at the last moment, boarded the Washington–New York shuttle.

The Senator, a friend of many years' standing, had been deeply offended. Tracy had contributed heavily to the Senator's next campaign fund, but things had never really been the same between them since.

Trace handed the empty glass out under the door of the booth. "One more, sweetheart," he said, "and Old Dad will be just fine."

* * * * *

Harvey Bernstein collapsed in the window seat and was asleep by the time they were airborne.

The stewardess, rolling the drink table down the aisle, appeared to be close to orgasm. "Guess who's on board?" she said to Cathy.

"Tracy Steele," Cathy said.

"*Tracy Steele!*" the stewardess said.

"Double vodka and ice," Cathy said.

"What about *him?*" the stewardess asked, indicating with some revulsion the sleeping Harvey.

"The same."

"*Tracy Steele!*" the stewardess said again and closed her eyes in ecstasy.

Cathy took the four itty-bitty bottles of vodka and slipped them into her bag. "You forgot the vodka," she said.

"Sorry," the stewardess said and passed her four more itty-bitty bottles.

You never knew when a plane was going to be grounded in Kansas City at two o'clock in the morning. Everybody, no matter how well adjusted, has his or her own superstitious fears about air travel. And takes the necessary precautions.

* * * * *

"If I were you, son," the technicolor Tracy said on the itty-bitty Technicolor screen, "I'd just drop that gun and come along nice and quiet."

Cathy yawned.

She disliked Westerns. Harvey was asleep. And there was work to be done. Quietly she picked up her bag and, ducking under the flickering image, moved up the aisle and into the lounge.

Trace and Tiger were seated across from each other playing gin. The stewardess was seated next to Trace leaning over him, studying his hand and breathing heavily. Tiger drew a jack and discarded the gin card he'd been sitting with for the past two minutes. Losing even one hand at gin made old Trace break out in a nasty rash.

"What the hell," Trace said. "Live dangerously. I'll go down with nine."

"Son of a bitch," Tiger said, "got me again!"

"Is this seat taken?" Cathy said to the stewardess.

The stewardess looked up and glared.

Cathy smiled.

Trace looked up, vaguely recognized Cathy, and grinned. "Well, sweetheart," he said. "Long time no see."

"We made a movie together once," Cathy said.

"So we did," Trace said. "So we did. I almost didn't recognize you with your clothes on." It was one of the regular jokes he made when he couldn't remember a young lady's name or where or when they had met.

Cathy knew he didn't recognize her and was delighted.

The stewardess rose. Trace caught her arm.

"Sweetheart," Trace said, "how about bringing us three vodka stingers?"

"Sorry, Mr. Steele," she said coldly. "Two drinks to a customer. CAB regulations." She flounced off to the lavatory and closed the door behind her. It wasn't much of an exit, but it was the best she could manage without actually opening the cabin door and throwing herself out onto Reading, Pennsylvania, 30,000 feet below.

Cathy slid into her seat, opened her bag, and took out four of the itty-bitty vodka bottles, placing two in front of Trace and two in front of Tiger.

"We aim to please," Cathy said.

"Baby," Trace said, "you are a beautiful thing."

Tiger opened the bottles and poured the vodka over the melting ice in their empty glasses.

"Your deal, Trace," Tiger said.

Cathy opened her bag and took out one of the paperbacks she had bought at the newsstand. It happened to be
Philosophy in the Bedroom by the Marquis de Sade. It was in
dialogue and easy to read. She had just reached the part where
Eugénie was explaining the various erogenous zones when the
impecably dressed young man with the Afro hairdo and the
Colt .45 ducked politely under the movie screen and entered
the lounge.

"Good evening," the young man said. "This is your
new captain speaking. Our flying time to Havana will be
six hours and twenty-two minutes. If we all remain calm and
love each other, no one will be hurt." He bowed politely to
Tracy. "A pleasure to have you on board, Mr. Steele. I've
admired you on the screen ever since I was a little boy. More
recently I've seen a number of your older films on television.
They stand up very nicely."

"Well, gee, thanks," Tracy said.

"Now if you sit quietly and continue your game, all
will be well." He glanced briefly at Tiger's cards.

"You dumb whitey bastard," he said, not unkindly.
He reached into Tiger's hand and discarded the eight Tiger
had just drawn. "Gin," the young man said, then turned,
walked to the cockpit, and opened the door.

"Don't be alarmed, gentlemen," he said, holding the
gun at the pilot's head. "They tell me Cuba is especially lovely
this time of year." Then he closed the door.

Tracy Steele's face was ashen.

He felt his stomach lurch.

"How can I go to Cuba?" he said. "I got a meeting
at the studio at ten-thirty in the morning."

Cathy got out the other four itty-bitty vodka bottles,
opened them herself, and passed them one at a time to Trace.
He drank them in eight easy gulps.

Then she reached into the bag and produced Harvey's gun.

"Why don't you just go up there and take him?" she said.

"What?" Tracy said.

"Me?" Tracy said.

"Why?" Tracy said.

"You have a meeting at the studio tomorrow morning," Cathy said. "Besides, think of the publicity. 'Movie Star Tracy Steele Saves Hijacked Plane.'"

"The kid's right," Tiger said. "It's a hell of a gimmick."

"They wouldn't say: 'Movie Star Tracy Steele.' They'd just say: TRACY STEELE. Everybody knows I'm a movie star. They only put 'Movie Star' in front of somebody's name with kids you never heard of. Real movie stars, all they need is the name itself. Why don't *you* take him, Tiger?"

Tiger was beginning to enjoy himself for the first time in eleven years.

"Jeez, Trace," he said, "I'd love to. But, I mean, how would it *look?* 'Tracy Steele's *Dialogue Director* Saves Hijacked Plane'? What kind of shit is that?"

"We could *tell* the papers I did it."

"Witnesses. The pilots and everybody. I don't think we could make it stick," Tiger said.

Trace looked at Cathy.

She shook her head.

Trace shrugged. The four itty-bitty bottles of vodka had just hit bottom.

"Well, maybe you're right," he said. "What do you think I should do?"

"Go up there," Tiger said, "open the door, and stick the lady's gun up against the back of his head."

"Then what? I got to *say* something. I got to have some kind of dialogue."

Cathy said, "Why don't you try, 'If I were you, son, I'd just drop that gun and come along nice and quiet.' "

"Sure, Trace," Tiger said. "You can remember that. You said it in your last picture."

Tracy considered the matter carefully.

"What time is it in California?" he said. "I mean there's no point in getting my ass shot off if we miss the early edition of the LA *Times*."

"This is not just LA, Trace," Tiger said. "This is big. Every wire service in the world will be waiting when we hit the airport. TV cameras. Telstar. Christ, when you hit the studio tomorrow morning they'll be shitting all over themselves."

"Okay," Tracy said. "I'll do it. I just have to take a crap first."

"Oh, for God's sake," Cathy said. "Come on!" She pulled Tracy to his feet, led him to the cabin door, and put the gun in his hand.

"Okay, action!" she said, yanking the cabin door open with one hand and shoving Tracy forward with the other.

"If I were you, son," the internationally famous voice droned, "I'd just drop that gun and come along nice and quiet."

The flight engineer, against whose head Tracy had pressed the P-38, dropped the revolver he was holding against the young hijacker's head and slowly raised his hands.

"My God," the pilot said wearily, without taking his eyes from the controls, "where do *you* want to go?"

"LA," Tracy said. "I have a meeting at the studio at ten o'clock tomorrow morning."

Even the young hijacker was impressed.

"If my Cuban plans have been foiled," he said, "could I at least have your autograph?"

"I thought you'd never ask," Tracy said. That was

another of his standard jokes. One he used to demonstrate humility in the presence of his fans.

"Would you mind making it out to my wife? She's back in tourist."

Tracy grinned his one-million-against-ten-per-cent-of-the-gross grin, handed the P-38 to the flight engineer, and reached for his fountain pen.

*   *   *   *   *

Cathy mixed herself a double vodka and ice from the unguarded drink table, waved a polite good night to Tiger, who, for reasons of his own, appeared to be convulsed with laughter, and made her way back to her seat. Harvey was still sleeping. She kissed him gently on the brow and sat there for a while in the darkness, sipping her drink and making plans for their future.

2

The Los Angeles International Airport, which is usually quiet at one o'clock in the morning, was jammed. Two press conferences (separate but equal) were being held simultaneously. At one Trace was explaining how he had single-handedly disarmed the crazed hijacker. At the other the crazed hijacker sat silently while his wife of one day held forth on the subject of her husband's martyrdom. While her husband was in jail, she explained, she would occupy her time by writing a book on the black-power movement and the joys of inter-racial marriage.

Had she ever written anything before, a reporter asked.

No, she said, but her father, a famous teacher of creative writing at The Best-Selling Writers School in Condon Heights, Connecticut, would certainly help her.

Cathy led the still dazed Harvey through the crowds.

There were no taxis to be had but, naturally since Tracy was on the plane, there was a limousine standing by.

"Mr. Steele's car?"

The driver nodded.

"The Beverly Hills Hotel," Cathy said.

The driver stared at her.

Cathy stared back.

She had been hijacking limousines longer than the driver (a temporarily unemployed actor) had been driving them.

"Yes, ma'am," he finally said.

Harvey was asleep once more with his head in Cathy's lap as the limousine drove off into the black Los Angeles night.

Chapter SEVEN

1

Harvey Bernstein's "suicide" came as a surprise to no one. "Inevitable" was the word most often used by those of his friends who bothered to comment at all. "Tragic," they said, "but inevitable."

"He used to get pissed at cocktail parties and start playing with this absolutely *sinister* gun," said the bare-midriffed wife of one of his neighbors. "I never thought he'd have the guts to do it, though. Of course, he'd killed God knows how many people during the war."

His former secretary, Miss Akron, was the first to bring his absence to the attention of anyone even remotely in authority.

"Mr. Bernstein hasn't come to the office for a couple of days now," she reported to his immediate superior at The Best-Selling Writers School.

"Maybe you ought to call his house or something," his immediate superior had said.

Miss Akron had done so.

She got Mrs. Edwards on the phone. Mrs. Edwards had forgotten that her employment had been terminated. She had a vague recollection of a series of conversations that she might

or might not have had with Harvey. She had been making a
second batch of frozen daiquiris in the Waring Blendor when
the phone rang.

"Is he there?" Miss Akron had said.

"Who dat?" Mrs. Edwards had said.

It had been another one of those conversations.

Thoroughly shaken, Miss Akron had gone back to Harvey's cubicle, unlocked the locked drawer of his desk, and
found the almost empty vodka bottle, the picture of Cathy, and
the suicide note.

She burst into tears. Not because she *felt* anything.
It just seemed to be the thing to do.

"He's killed himself," she said to his immediate superior. "He's taken his own life."

"Tragic but inevitable," his immediate superior said.
"Maybe we should call the police or something."

"Would that be wise?" Miss Akron said. "We have the
school to think of."

"Quite so, quite so." There was about two fingers
(pinkies) left in the bottom of the vodka bottle. He emptied
the bottle into his coffee cup and drained it. He examined the
photograph of Cathy thoughtfully and then put it into his desk
drawer.

"How long have you been with us, Miss . . . ?"

"Akron. Eleanor Akron. Almost three and a half
years."

"Ah, yes. Do you think you could handle his work load?
I mean, you must be familiar with his students. Their progress,
their development. That sort of thing."

"I'd love to try," Eleanor Akron said.

In due course a cable had been dispatched to Margery
and Max in Europe and a telegram had been sent to his son at
Berkeley.

"I know it's ridiculous," Margery had said, "but I feel almost *guilty*." They were seated, sipping Campari and soda on the terrace of the Gritti Palace. They had ordered a gondola for eleven-thirty, but it had not yet showed up. "No wonder Venice is sinking," Max had been saying. "It is sinking under the weight of American tourists."

"And the Germans," Margery had said.

"And their goddamned cameras," Max had said.

Max and Margery were, if truth be known, ideally suited. They shared all the right prejudices. At least, put it another way, they deplored all the correct things. "It is not possible for a Black Panther to get a fair trial in America today!" they would whisper into each other's ear at moments of climax. It was their "ointment."

"Particularly if he shot someone in the belly in the presence of witnesses," Harvey would have whispered back had he been present, which fortunately he was not.

They also felt strongly about Indians, air pollution, overpopulation, Mace, and, in Max's case, the unfairness of the graduated income tax as it applied to artists who might make three hundred grand in *one* year and then not see another cent until the movie rights were sold.

"I suppose we ought to do something," Margery said. "You know, like make *arrangements*."

"What sorts of arrangements?"

"Well, there's the house."

"It's yours now. You could turn it over to the Unwed Mothers' Association. Harvey would have wanted that."

"And there should probably be some sort of memorial service."

"Why?" Max said.

"I don't know, actually," Margery said.

Then the gondola arrived to take them to see the glassblowers. "Harvey loved Venice," Margery said, blowing her nose in Harvey's memory. "He always said it reminded him of Atlantic City."

Bernie (he could not bear to be called Bruce) turned white and then recovered quickly.

"What is it?"

"The old man's knocked himself off. Gone to that great Smirnoff Factory In The Sky."

"Tough."

"Yeah."

"You think he left any bread?"

"You must be kidding."

There was a three-inch obituary on page twenty-six of *The New York Times*. Harvey was referred to as a "critic," and the only fact about his forty-six years of life that the *Times* had seen fit to print was that he had been the only critic to write unfavorably of Philip Roth's *Goodbye, Columbus,* which was referred to (erroneously) as a novel. Actually, it was a novella and five short stories.

Miss Akron continued to sign the lessons HB. It seemed easier that way. Neither Mrs. Mortimer, the General, nor Charles Douglas Potter appeared to notice the difference.

If his passing caused anything at all, it was a sigh. A sigh, perhaps, of relief.

Harvey had, toward the end, become something of a problem to everyone.

2

Cathy awoke filled with joy and silent laughter. Waves of happiness like little electric shocks tingled through her body. She propped herself up on one elbow and studied the sleeping Harvey. His face in repose (she decided) was actually *beautiful*. Dark and vaguely mysterious in a jazzy, Old Testament way. (Grandpa had greatly enjoyed reading aloud from the Bible when in his cups.) There was strength, she felt, beneath the little lines of pain. And untapped wells of tenderness, aching to be released. Her mind, of course, did not form those exact words. But the idea was there. *God, she actually thought, how lucky am I, after years of balling shits and studs and shits again, to wind up here, in this bed, in this hundred-and-twenty-dollar-a-day hotel suite, truly loving and being truly loved by this beautiful, intelligent, groovy man!*

"I was born," Cathy said aloud, gently nudging him with her elbow. "I awoke," she said, giving him a further nudge. "He plunged it into me," she added hopefully.

Harvey the Beautiful did not stir.

"All possible beginnings," she said, no longer able to contain her laughter, her joy. "But which? One hundred words, you silly son of a bitch! Shall I now describe to you in *five* hundred words the single most transcending experience of my life? Using one side of the page only?"

God, how I love you! she added silently.

Harvey the Strong, Harvey the Tender, Harvey the *Exhausted* moved not a muscle.

She kissed him lightly and slipped quietly out of bed.

It was a glorious morning.

Moving as silently as possible, she pulled on her pants and shirt, took the room key from the dresser, hung the DO NOT DISTURB sign on the outer knob, and started down the long, empty corridor toward the lobby.

For some reason the hotel seemed curiously deserted. In the Lower Arcade she stopped at the drugstore and bought sunglasses, a tube of Bain de Soleil, and a copy of the *Hollywood Reporter*. All of which, with a flash of her key, she charged to their room.

In a shop window at the end of the Arcade, a gold lamé bikini caught her eye.

The elderly redheaded saleslady could not have been nicer. Cathy was (she said) her first customer in weeks. She (the elderly redheaded saleslady) even let her split the sizes. A ten bottom and a twelve top. Together they admired it in the dressing-room mirror. It was a little *too* Las Vegas–Miami-hooker for Cathy's taste. But she figured Harvey could use a little Las Vegas–Miami-hookerdom in his life at the moment. Actually, she looked sensational in it, as most real ladies do when vulgarly attired.

She signed the tab ($32.95), put her pants and shirt into a pink-and-green paper shopping bag, and made her way down the steps toward the pool.

There was no attendant at the gate. Just a stack of towels on his desk. She took one and pattered, barefoot and shimmering, down the remaining steps.

The clock above the changing rooms said quarter to ten.

She was entirely alone.

It was all, suddenly, a little eerie.

Where, she wondered, were the blue-haired wives of the visiting exhibitors? Why were there no poolside breakfast meetings in progress? No Morris Office agents? No clients? No thunk of tennis balls from the nearby courts? Where the hell *was* everybody? This was the *pool* at the Beverly Hills Hotel, for Christ's sake! The red-hot center, the very *heart* of the nation's fourth largest and certainly most glamorous industry.

She carefully placed her towel and her packages on a table, walked to the edge of the pool, and tentatively poked one toe into the water.

Delicious!

The gold lamé bikini was, however, clearly designed for poolside lounging (i.e., attracting high-rolling Las Vegas winners who might wish entertainment at a hundred dollars a shot later in the evening). It was certainly not intended for swimming.

But the water sang its siren song.

What the hell!

She took a quick look around.

She was out of the bikini in a flash. Two flashes, actually. Then, a deep breath and a shallow dive. She swam the entire length underwater, made a racing turn at the deep end, and got back almost to the middle before it became necessary to come up for air.

It was so beautiful!

Everything!

To be Cathy! To love! To *be* loved! To be swimming naked and alone in the pool at the Beverly Hills Hotel at ten minutes to ten in the morning under a cloudless sky! For a moment or two she trod water, laughing and running her hands through her wet hair. It was a moment for poetry. She spoke, in triumph between giggles and gasps, the first lines that came to her mind.

> "There was an Old Woman
> Who lived in a shoe,
> And she can kiss my fucking ass too!"

Then, very deliberately, she swam six lengths, counting them off, pleased with herself, pleased with the glory of her body, pleased by the fact that she was only slightly winded when she finally pulled herself onto the steps at the shallow end.

She lay for a time on one of the chaises, permitting the sun the pleasure of drying the water on her skin. In a lifetime devoted almost entirely to physical gratification it was, perhaps, the most pleasurably sensual five minutes of her life.

Still naked (*I'm Cathy The Super-Girl! I'm Cathy The Invisible Woman! Call Me Monte Cristo! The World*

Is Mine!), she walked to the nearest telephone extension.

"Room service," she said.

A motherly voice answered.

She gave their room number. "I would like to order breakfast."

"Certainly, dear."

She had been away for a while and had thus forgotten that all the young-old old ladies in Southern California wore their hair dyed a bright red and called everybody "dear."

It was all so *right!* So *beautiful!*

"What would you like, dear?"

"We are in love," Cathy said, "and we have been fucking steadily for the last thirty-six hours. I have just swum six lengths naked in your glorious pool. What would you suggest, dear?"

"Goodness, dear," the divine red-haired housemother said, "you must be terribly hungry!"

"We are ravaged by hunger, dear," Cathy said.

"There was a time, dear," Red said, "when I too was young and in love. We fucked a great deal, of course, but in those days the Depression hung over the land like a great cloud of what we today have come to call smog. We could never *afford* the breakfast of our dreams."

"What, dear, would have been the breakfast of your dreams? Had there been no Depression and could you have ordered what you wished?"

"Orange juice and champagne, dear, in equal parts, served in tall ice-filled glasses with the champagne bottle waiting impatiently in a silver bucket to one side. Then, loosely scrambled eggs, smoked salmon, caviar, bagels (split, toasted, and thinly spread with unsalted butter), cream cheese, and gallons of hot, freshly made coffee."

"It sounds yummy, dear."

"Doesn't it, though? Oh, God, how poor Harry (rest

his soul) would have relished such a breakfast! I only hope, dear, that you, in the first blush of your carnal love, enjoy it as much as poor Harry and I might have."

"We will! We will! But tell them, please, to hurry!"

"You bet your ass, dear!" said the absolutely super red-haired old broad without missing a beat.

You can always tell a first-class hotel by the enthusiasm of its room service.

Cathy slipped (Flash! Flash!) back into her golden thirty-two-dollar-and-ninety-five-cent bikini, picked up her packages, and raced back barefoot through the empty hotel to Harvey, to their suite, and to breakfast.

3

When Jack Maybry smiled (which was often) his entire *person* lit up. His many teeth flashed. His eyes twinkled merrily, emitting rays of warmth that glowed with sincerity and understanding. When he was *really* angry (as he was now), the malted milk of human kindness that spilled from him was so thick you could eat it with a spoon.

At the age of fifty-seven, he could have passed for a youngish thirty-five. Since taking over the Studio (he was the third Vice-President-in-Charge-of-Production to have held that post in the past year), he had changed his image slightly.

Gone was the graying crew cut. Gone were the charcoal suits and the severe black knit ties. His raven locks now hung in clusters over the back collar of his cowboy shirt. Sideburns laddered his tanned cheeks. He rode to the Studio each morning on his motorbike. He had toyed with the idea of a beard, but in the end had decided against it as it tended to hide the radiance of his smile. He surveyed the room now with a beautific gaze unequaled since the late Pope John presided over his last ecumenical council.

His clear blue eyes caught and held Tracy Steele's slightly bloodshot ones for a fifteen-second love-in.

"Where the fuck," he said in his strawberry-shortcake voice, "was that dumb fucker Tiger during all this? *That's* what I don't understand. You, you stupid bastard! We *expect* you to step on your cock every time you open your dumb-actor mouth. We're *prepared* for it! That's why we never let you out of the fucking Studio gates without a fucking *keeper!* Jesus, I don't know why I have to do every fucking thing around here myself!"

He rose, beaming, from behind his desk, crossed the room, and fondly tousled Tracy's hair. "One lousy grandstand play, just one, and, single-*handed*, you lose us every pimply-faced little jerk-off fart under thirty in the *country! Plus* a potential audience of Christ knows how many spades who only go to the movies because they don't know how to turn *on* a television set *after* they've looted one!"

He turned to the Head of West Coast Publicity. "You think it's too late for Trace to issue some kind of public apology?"

The Head of West Coast Publicity shrugged. "We've been running polls all night. The stuff's just beginning to come out of the computer." He pulled some papers from his breast pocket. "I can't guarantee it yet down to the last fractional percentile because of the time difference factor, but it looks like eighty-six-point-seven per cent of white, college-educated Americans with annual incomes of seventy-five hundred or better tend to feel that a member of an oppressed minority group has every *right* to hijack a commercial aircraft during any time period in which it is being exploited for profit. When you figure in the high-school kids, the dropouts (they're a little tough to poll, most of them don't have phones), undergraduate students and, of course, the coons themselves, it's going to run a lot higher. Maybe ninety-one, ninety-two per cent."

"Jeez, Jack," Tracy said, "I'm sorry. As a matter of

fact, I was scared shitless. I just did it because I thought it would be good for my image."

"Sure, baby," Jack said, patting Trace reassuringly on the shoulder. But his mind had already moved on to other, more important matters.

He crossed thoughtfully back to his desk and flicked a button on his IBM Interoffice Communicator. "Get hold of Tiger," he said, "and tell him get his ass down to the LA County jail. Tell him to see if the kid, Leslie, or whatever his dumb coon name is, needs anything. Then get hold of Legal and tell them the Studio is ready to stand bail." He turned to Publicity. "Make sure all releases make one thing clear: Tracy was acting totally on his own. The Studio in no way approves or condones his hasty and ill-advised antisocial behavior." He flicked the button once again. "Telex New York and tell them I want all Steele films pulled out of current release." He turned to Tracy. "Just a safety measure, sweetheart," he said. "No point in having a lot of theaters bombed. Not that militant minorities don't have every *right* to bomb theaters showing films that tend to denigrate their human dignity. But you know how it is. Look, baby, why don't you just beat it down to the Springs or someplace for a while. Stay out of sight. Maybe we can figure out a way to square all this."

Thus dismissed, Tracy Steele left the office, walked the length of the deserted studio street to the parking lot, empty except for his 365 GTBY (two place, 404 liter, 4 cam engine– 5 speed synco, acceleration capability zero to one hundred m.p.h. in six seconds) Ferrari. Thoughtfully he pulled on his Hermes racing gloves, adjusted his helmet and goggles, and slid into the car. It was only then that he remembered that Tiger was not there and he did not know how to drive.

He burst into tears.

Later, after a couple of drinks in his empty twelve-room dressing-room-office suite in the Emmenthal Building—offices that were soon to be turned into a commune for the younger contract players and their illegitimate offspring—Tracy walked to the gate and had one of the studio cops call him a cab. He went directly to the empty Bistro (of which he was a part owner) and sat alone at the bar for a very long time.

After the fourth martini his sadness slowly turned to rage. He began to wonder whether one of his corporations, perhaps the one that owned the six restaurants, might not be well-advised to add a motion-picture company to its extensive list of holdings.

*   *   *   *   *

Later that afternoon, at a hastily called press conference, Smiling Jack delivered his now famous dictum that was published everywhere and got him, the following week, the cover of *Time* magazine.

The Big Star system is hereby declared officially dead, was what Jack-baby said in effect. No longer would a young and beautiful audience be subjected to the vulgarity of watching middle-aged, grotesque-looking (and, he did not add, highly priced) movie actors such as Tracy Steele, Burt Lancaster, Elizabeth Taylor, Kirk Douglas, Deborah Kerr, etc., etc., groping each other on the silver screen.

4

That these irrelevant (and somewhat dopey) remarks were to set in motion the preposterous series of events that would ultimately catapult Harvey Bernstein into a position of honor in the great Galaxy of American Comic Folk Heroes (persons who make, or have made, such spectacular public asses of themselves that their fellow citizens begin to find them *endearing* and finally end up immortalizing them; their numbers include a twelve-times-married playboy, four-star general, a family of Hungarian hookers, a major novelist with political ambitions, a Women's Lib leader, a hippie quarterback, a Vice-President of the United States, and to bring it down to a purely local level, the guy across the street who has started *bragging* that he once bought an Edsel) was, of course, something that no one could have predicted at the time.

Certainly not Cathy and Harvey.

Breakfast had been a great success. They had ordered a second bottle of champagne, drunk most of it, made love, gone for a walk, and were now back in the suite, undressing for dinner.

"Breakfast," Harvey said, "was $143.75 plus tip. I really don't think we can afford to stay in this hotel forever."

"Of course not. Tomorrow we start looking for a house."

"But what happens when the money runs out?"

"By that time you'll have taught me to be a Best-Selling Writer."

Harvey had forgotten about *that*. His heart sank. But only briefly.

"Now, shall I order dinner?" Cathy said, pulling her shirt over her head. "Or would you rather wait a little while?"

They waited a little while.

*　*　*　*　*

In fact, they did not get around to looking at houses (or making Cathy a Best-Selling Writer) for almost a week.

There was so much to see and do.

They made love and then lunched at the Brown Derby on Vine Street, failing, so engrossed in each other were they, to notice that they were the only customers in the place.

They made love and then dined at the ultra-exclusive Bistro in Beverly Hills and were filled with awe and wonder at the genuineness of its exclusivity. With eight captains, sixteen waiters, thirty-two busboys, and three barmen at the service of but a single couple, it seemed even grander than Cathy remembered it.

They made love and then went to The Factory. When Harvey complained that the volume of recorded music made conversation impossible, someone (he appeared to be one of the owners) apologized and, after a considerable search, put on an old Glenn Miller album for them. They danced happily cheek to cheek in the empty discotheque until closing time.

They made love and then took a guided tour of movie stars' homes. While there were no movie stars in evidence, one house in particular caught Cathy's eye. A rambling mansion in Holmby Hills. "Now *that* would be absolutely perfect for us!" Cathy said.

They made love and then they visited a movie studio, which proved slightly disappointing. They had hoped to see a picture actually being filmed. But as there was nothing shooting in Hollywood at the moment, they were forced to settle for a tour of the back lot and a quick look-in at the New Talent School, where a group of "stars of the future" sat huddled together for warmth, apparently picking fleas out of each other's hair.

5

"Do we *really* have to go to Disneyland?" Harvey said.

They were drinking champagne and orange juice, but in a lunatic (and fortunately only passing) attempt at economy they had knocked off the caviar for breakfast. They were getting bored with caviar anyway. "It's just another kind of eggs," Cathy had said. "I don't know why certain things are okay for certain meals and not okay for others. I don't see why you can't have anything you want any time you want it."

"That," Harvey had said, "is a question the human race has been asking since the moment it came swinging down from the trees. Which was," he added, "in the broad spectrum of history a fairly recent and not, perhaps, totally desirable event."

"What I've always wanted," Cathy had said, "was about ten orders of mashed potatoes served on a great big platter with a pound of butter sunk in the middle and lots of pieces of crisp Canadian bacon around the edges. The idea is, you don't use forks or anything. You just scoop up the potatoes with the bacon."

Like many people whose line of work requires them to keep an eye on their weight, she was obsessed by the idea of potatoes in all forms. She also had a thing about spaghetti, especially eaten cold from the refrigerator on hangover mornings.

"Of course we don't have to go," Cathy said in answer to Harvey's question about Disneyland. "Actually, it's kind of like Las Vegas. Except that one is Heaven and the other is Hell."

"Which is which?" Harvey said.

"I don't know," Cathy said. "But when I die I sure God hope I wind up in Vegas."

They were, in some ways (not many), like an old married couple. Seated across from each other at the room-service breakfast table, Cathy was reading the *Wall Street Journal* and Harvey had the waiter steal him a two-day-old copy of *The New York Times*.

"A friend of mine once advised me," Cathy said, shoveling a Canadian bacon load of mashed potatoes mouthward, "to put my savings in AT&T. Thank God I kept them in the YWCA. It was selling at sixty-eight at the time. It closed yesterday at forty-four and five-eighths."

Harvey, who had not seen a *New York Times* for a week, turned automatically, as was his custom, to the obituary page.

Harvey Bernstein, Critic, the minuscule headline at the
bottom of page twenty-six read. If you've ever seen your own
name in print, you know how vividly it jumps out at you.
Except, probably, in the case of your obituary.

Harvey scanned the short paragraph (reading time: 9
seconds) carefully. It seemed to be mostly about Philip Roth.

"You're wrong," he said to Cathy at length. "It's not
just a Disneyland/Las Vegas situation. It's obviously more
complicated than that. Is it possible that the Beverly Hills
Hotel is God's Fort Dix? A way station, a form of Divine
Purgatory to which you are temporarily posted while awaiting
permanent assignment?"

"What the fuck are you talking about?" Cathy said.
She was trying to do something about her language, but sometimes Harvey's circumlocutions got on her nerves.

Harvey passed her *The New York Times.*

Cathy studied the paper for a moment, frowning.

"What have you got against Philip Roth?" Cathy said.

"Nothing. On a professional level, I admire Phil
extravagantly. I was, at the time, simply jealous of his success. What depressed me most, I think, was his ability to release
from the Potash—and Perlmutter, if you will—of ethnic humor
a shower of neutrons of purest plutonium."

"What does that mean?"

"Nothing. Like my three hundred and ninety-nine other
reviews. Listen, I'll be goddamned if I'm going to sit here
on the morning of my own demise discussing Philip *Roth!*"

He rose, walked to the writing table, and began to
scribble a note.

"What are you doing?"

"Composing a letter to the *Times* informing them that
the reports of my death have been grossly understated."

"I don't even know what *that* means!"

"Sartre has told us that Hell is other people. He did not, however, suggest that the other people would be a beautiful blonde without a stitch of clothes or a shred of literary reference. But then, of course, M. Sartre had never visited either Las Vegas or Disneyland."

For some reason he was suddenly in high good spirits.

"You know what I think?" he said, tearing his letter to the *Times* into little pieces which he then threw in the air like confetti. "I think the dumb sons of bitches found my suicide note and really think I'm *dead!*"

Cathy's eyes widened. She was beginning to catch on.

"What about your wife and What's-his-name in wherever they are? Shouldn't you wire them or something?" she said, crossing her fingers *and* toes (no easy trick unless you are supple and extremely young: 18, 19, 20, 21, 22, 23, 24— choose one), hoping for the right answer.

"Wire Max and Margery in Venice? Are you mad? Let sleeping Doges lie!"

Although the joke was not very good, it was the right answer. She threw her arms around him.

"Don't you want to finish your breakfast first?"

"I love cold mashed potatoes. They're even better than cold spaghetti!"

* * * * *

"And you won't ever leave me? You won't ever have to go back?"

"How can I go back? I'm dead!"

"Not all *that* dead."

"Pretty dead."

"Pretty, yes. Dead, no. . . . And we can rent a house and live like *real* people?"

"I'm not real people. I'm a ghost. The ghost of Christmas Past."

Cathy snuggled closer to him.

"Maybe we can have a Christmas tree and everything. A wonderful pink one, set up by the pool . . ."

Chapter EIGHT

1

The Real Estate Lady had long, tanned legs, long, tanned arms, tangerine-colored hair, flashing white teeth, six gold charm bracelets, and a broken heart.

She had recently been divorced by a television star whose series had been canceled. As is the local custom among recently divorced wives of ex-television stars, she had gone into Real Estate. The tennis pro whom her husband had most unchivalrously named in the divorce proceedings, thereby cutting her out of a handsome community property settlement, had blown the duke by not only billing her husband for "lessons" but adding, imprudently as it turned out, a charge of $37.50 for "balls." That was, as she herself was the first to admit, when the shit really hit the fan.

They were approaching the fifteenth house she had shown them that morning. Thus far Cathy had found nothing that could be deemed totally suitable. The Real Estate Lady was on the verge of tears when she accidentally made the wrong turn off Hanover onto Carolwood Drive and there it was! The house they had seen on the tour. "That's the one," Cathy said.

"How do you know it's for rent?" Harvey said.

"Everything is for rent," the Real Estate Lady said,
brightening perceptibly. "You can't imagine what it's like in
this town."

She fumbled through her notes, and sure enough, the
house had come on the market two weeks before.

"It's the old John Barrymore house," she said as she
had been taught to say about any house of more than ten
rooms in which a client seemed even vaguely interested.

"Actually, the present owner is . . ." She hesitated a
moment. "I'm not supposed to say, but his name is a Household Word. He doesn't want it to get around that the place is
on the market. He's off in Yugoslavia or someplace making a
Western. He'll let it go for nothing—say a thousand a month
on a six-month lease provided the tenant keeps up the staff.
And provided we have the right to show it to potential buyers.
With proper notice, of course."

"A staff!" Cathy said. "It comes with a staff?" She
seemed delighted by the idea.

"Two full-time gardeners, a pool man three times a
week, a chef, a housemaid, a secretary, and a best friend," she
said.

"*A best friend?*" Harvey said.

The brokenhearted Real Estate Lady with the superb
backhand she could no longer afford to use nodded. "All movie
stars whose names are household words have Best Friends,"
she explained, pulling the Thunderbird to a halt under the
porte-cochere.

The house—a mansion, really—was of no known archi-
tecture. Protected from the street by electric gates and a high
stone wall and fronted by an acre or two of Technicolor lawn,
the building itself was surrounded by a cluster of man-made
jungle.

"The pool is in the back." The Real Estate Lady was
reading from a mimeographed sheet. "The pool house is

equipped with indoor-outdoor barbecue, wet bar, sauna, and flagellation room. I think that's what it says."

Cathy clapped her hands with pleasure. "What do you think?" she said to Harvey.

Harvey thought it was twenty minutes to one and if he didn't get a drink pretty soon the top of his head was going to come off. "I think maybe we should see the inside," he said. "And possibly you will want to interview the staff."

The Real Estate Lady pressed the doorbell.

Somewhere within a chime chimed.

Presently the door opened.

The young man who opened it was tall, with long, sun-streaked surfer's hair, and was tanned to the color (Harvey thought, his tongue hanging out) of a Scotch old-fashioned. He was clad in skintight, much-faded baby-blue denims, the ends of which hung in interestingly frayed tatters just below his bronzed knees. His bare chest was hairless. His pectorals were lean but rocklike. His left wrist was encircled by a serpent-shaped bracelet.

"Hi," he said.

"Hi," Cathy said.

"I'm Ken," the young man said.

"I'm Cathy." They seemed to come immediately to some secret understanding.

"I'm sure we'll be great friends," Ken said.

"I'm sure," Cathy said.

The Real Estate Lady looked at Ken and experienced a definite twinge. Without her being aware of it, he reminded her of her tennis player, which was perfectly natural as he was pretty much the same person. In the sense that there are only one hundred original people in the world, the rest being signed, numbered lithographs of one of the originals. Her tennis player had been number 6999 in an edition of 7000. Ken *was* 7000. The bottom of the Warren Beatty barrel. After him, of course, came endless thousands of unsigned, unnumbered prints, slightly smudged but suitable for framing. Anyway, that was the reason for the attraction. Ken recognized the Real Estate Lady at once, remembered the unhappy details of her divorce settlement, and immediately turned his attention to Harvey.

"I would very much like a drink," Harvey said.

"We're just making Bloodys," Ken said. "Veronica!" he shouted over his shoulder. "Veronica *X*, you get your black ass in here this minute!"

He led them through the marbled entrance hall. "Down home," he said to Harvey, "the darkies knew their place!"

"Where *I* come from," Veronica X said, entering dramatically through the French doors, "we cut faggots' balls off and eat them for breakfast. With cow cock and butter beans!" She was a spectacular-looking black girl with sopping-wet hair. She was wearing a sopping-wet watermelon-colored bikini.

"Just you stop dripping on the floor," Ken said. "It's bad enough that you *pee* in the pool!" He turned once again to Harvey. "You simply cannot *teach* them!" he said. "You *bus* them out of *Watts* at great *expense,* and the first thing you know, there they are, voiding their great black bladders in the swimming pool. It's Olympic size," he added, "and we keep it at a constant temperature of eighty degrees. Fahrenheit."

"Drink," Harvey said hoarsely. "I desperately need a drink."

"Your pleasure, sir?" Veronica X said.

"My pleasure is your pleasure," Harvey said.

"Her pleasure is peeing in the pool," Ken said. "The gentleman, however, would like a Bloody Mary."

"Me too," said Cathy.

"Me too," said the Real Estate Lady.

"That's four Bloody Marys, Veronica dear," Ken said. "And do try not to forget the celery salt. I think," he said, batting his eyelashes at Harvey, "that a *pinch* of celery salt makes *all* the difference."

"Why don't you have Juan Rodriguiz put a pinch of celery salt on the end of his *dicky?*" Veronica X said. "It would make *all* the *difference!*"

"You shut your big Ubangi mouth! Her parents, you know," he said to Harvey, "wore bones in their noses and had lips the size of toilet seats!"

"This is certainly a *remarkable* way to show a *house!*" the Real Estate Lady said.

"I've worked in houses," Veronica X said, "where the Best Friend wasn't even allowed to *mix* with the company!"

Harvey Bernstein, holding the top of his head in place with his left hand, disengaged himself from the group and, moving like a homing pigeon, headed off through a towering archway into the living room, the principle feature of which was an ornate, freestanding antique bar graced with a heartwarming array of bottles. The fact that the silver ice bucket was empty did not bother him in the least.

A few minutes later he was feeling well enough to rejoin the house-viewers in the lanai and be introduced to the rest of the indoor staff: Felix the chef and Miss Thuringer the secretary.

Felix was an ancient but still wiry Filipino who had bought, before emigrating to the mainland, Benguet Gold (a Philippine mining company presently quoted on the New York Stock Exchange at 12½) for five cents a share and was rich enough to buy and sell them all. He had toyed with the notion of renting the place himself after Household Word's enforced exile but had decided against it on the grounds that it might prejudice his monthly Social Security check. He was a sensational if arrogant cook, a great handicapper (better, for some reason, at Hollywood Park than at Santa Anita), and lusted mightily after the person of Veronica X, for whom he prepared special and outrageously expensive lunches. He had, for example, managed to convince her that caviar blinis (one of his specialties) were an advanced form of soul food. Some afternoon he would get her loaded enough (he had also convinced her that Dom Pérignon was a soft drink not unlike 7-Up) to lure her back to his lavishly appointed servant's quarters. . . .

Thus far she had resisted his advances with a series of wry chuckles. "Man," she would say while sipping the Dom through chocolate-tinted flavor straws, "you may be a four-foot-six yellow cat with a mouthful of gold teeth, but you sure are a *horny* little bastard!"

The hint of veiled admiration in her voice contained enough promise to keep him from going through with his frequently announced intention of buying one of the smaller hotels on the Las Vegas Strip and living out his remaining days in happy, well-earned retirement.

Miss Thuringer appeared on the surface to be of less interest (which only shows the folly of making snap character judgments on the basis of insufficient information). She had never, she told Cathy, worked with a writer before and found the prospect infinitely exciting.

They ran out of tomato juice rather early on, but there turned out to be plenty of ice, and after the second round, vodka on the rocks seemed easier anyway.

As far as Cathy was concerned, it was love at first sight. The whole thing: house, staff, pool, and flagellation room (which was actually a gym, Ken explained; the whips were simply left over from the days when it was still possible to keep horses in Holmby Hills. The chains were doubtless for the automobile tires in the event of a sudden but heavy snowfall in Southern California) was everything she had ever dreamed of. And more. The "more" was the bidet in the master bath.

Cathy had *heard* of them, of course, but had never

actually seen one before. On the pretext of having to powder her nose, she had given it a test run.

2

"I love it! I just love it!" Cathy said to Harvey. This was sometime later—now almost three o'clock in the afternoon. She and Harvey had locked themselves into the bathroom in order to experiment with the bidet under what Harvey chose to call "control conditions." He had consumed three quarters of a bottle of vodka and Cathy was a little high herself.

The Real Estate Lady had driven back to her office to collect the necessary papers, *just in case.* Ken had been dispatched to Beverly Hills for more tomato juice. Miss Thuringer was spending her lunch hour (as she usually did) seated in a variant of the lotus position before a small altar she had constructed in the abandoned nursery, muttering runic incantations and sticking pins in a wax effigy of Household Word. In the kitchen Felix was plying Veronica X with salmon mousse.

"What *is* this shit?" Veronica X was saying.

"Salmon mousse," Felix said. He was using a pair of pliers to untwist the cork, which is the only proper way to open a bottle of Dom if you have any regard for the balls of your thumbs.

"Salmon *what?*"

"Salmon *mousse.* The tender flesh of freshly poached salmon, pressed through a series of strainers and then souffléd."

"What a lousy thing to do to a salmon," Veronica X said with some feeling.

"Why don't you let me help you out of your wet things?" Felix said as the cork popped. He filled her Bugs Bunny glass with champagne and began to unfasten the hook at the back of her still-wet bikini top.

"You *are* a horny little bastard!" Veronica X said. But she let him undo her all the same.

* * * * *

What with one thing and another it seemed to Cathy
an ideal setting in which to become a Best-Selling Writer.

"But can we afford it?" Harvey said. He had wisely
brought another bottle of vodka up with them and was lying
flat on his back on the white-carpeted floor.

"I don't see why not," Cathy said. "I mean what's the
point of being a Best-Selling Writer if you don't live like one?"

"It's so big," Harvey said. "We'll rattle around."

"Not really," Cathy said. "We need a room for us,
right? And I think I'll want Veronica X to sleep in. It makes
so much more sense. Then, I'll need a room to work in. And
an office for Miss Thuringer. And maybe you'll want your children to visit from time to time."

"God forbid," Harvey said.

He was attempting to drink from the neck of the bottle
while lying flat on his back. He looked so sweet and cuddly and
innocent that Cathy couldn't stand it. Presently she joined him
on the floor.

"I think we should take the place," she said dreamily
sometime later. "It has the grooviest vibrations."

So they took it, naturally. On a six-month lease. Later
they all had a drink to celebrate.

Then Felix cooked dinner.

Then Ken drove over to the Beverly Hills Hotel, packed
their stuff (minimal), and checked them out.

After all, what are Best Friends for?

Chapter NINE

1

Cathy was all business.

"How long does it *take* to write a Best Seller?" she asked. They were seated by the pool the following morning.

"That depends."

"On what?"

"On a lot of things. On what *kind* of Best Seller you want to write, for instance."

"What kind of Best Sellers are there?"

"Basically, Best Sellers are divided into two categories: Fiction and Nonfiction."

Cathy nodded gravely. This was the sort of personalized instruction she had hoped to get when she first enrolled in The Best-Selling Writers School. She could not *believe* how divinely everything had worked out! "Go on," she said. "Fiction and Nonfiction?"

"In the area of Nonfiction, three themes generally predominate. Books that explain in simple, nontechnical language how to make a million dollars. Books that explain, in slightly more complicated terms, how to screw. And as-told-to autobiographies of illiterate persons who have attained national prominence either by their skill at making a million dollars or by their skill at screwing. For a time books by persons who had been employed in one capacity or another by the Kennedy family enjoyed a certain vogue. Although the form seems for the moment to have played itself out, I am constantly amazed that *anything at all* was accomplished in the White House, what with the First Lady's faggots measuring for slip covers and the rest of the staff continuously making notes for future Best Sellers. The din of the typewriters must have been overwhelming. To say nothing of the scratching of ball-point pens, the rustle of swatches, and the Xeroxing of laundry lists. It is my prayer that someday, among the late President's personal papers, there will be found a journal describing *his* views of his secretary, his cook, his chauffeur, the baby sitter, and the present Mrs. Onassis's then chiropodist. This is, perhaps, too much to hope for. But, Christ, what a publisher's wet dream! *My Life With My Secretary Who Happened To Be A Boring, Meddlesome, Gossip-Mongering Old Bitch Sorely In Need Of Typing Lessons: A Personal Memoir by JFK.*"

Harvey was beginning to warm up to his subject. "Or," he continued, "how about *The Cook Who Couldn't Boil An Egg: The Story Of An Unhappy Easter Sunday On The White House Lawn—by JFK?* The possibilities are endless!"

"I think maybe I'm more interested in Fiction," Cathy said, neatly heading him off at the pass. "Tell me about that."

Harvey took a deep breath.

"The choice is narrower," Harvey said. "There are thin sensitive novels or thick *in*sensitive ones. There appears to be no middle ground."

"Which is better?"

"Thick *in*sensitive ones."

"Why?"

"They sell for ten dollars a copy."

"What would happen if someone wrote a *thin in*sensitive novel?"

"More difficult, of course, but not impossible. There was a thin insensitive novel last year called *Love Story* that was able to achieve in a scant thirty thousand words a mind-boggling level of banality that would have taken a less experienced author at least two *hundred* thousand words even to approach."

There was a pause.

"You know what might be good?" Cathy said tentatively.

"A Bloody Mary," Harvey said.

"It's only ten-thirty. We made a deal you wouldn't start before eleven."

"True."

"No, really. What if someone wrote a thick insensitive novel about someone who *wanted* to make a million dollars and *wanted* to learn how to screw and in the book he *does* learn how to make a million dollars and *does* learn how to screw? That way we could get everything in. Maybe"—she was beginning to get excited now—"he could once have been President Kennedy's dentist or something, so we'd have that going for us too."

"It is no bad thing," Harvey said, more to himself than to Cathy, "to have a novel which is, indeed, *informed* by data of some sort, provided those data are of general interest. Mary McCarthy has said that one can learn to make strawberry jam from reading *Anna Karenina*."

"I don't know how to make strawberry jam," Cathy said, "but I know all about *Anna Karenina*. It's about a bunch of colored people in Harlem. Some friends of mine are making a movie of it."

Harvey could feel the top of his head beginning to come loose. But Cathy was undaunted. In fact, she was beginning to get hot.

"Is it all right to take a book that was written a long

time ago, like a classic, and change it around so that it's all
happening today?"

"Of course," Harvey said. "As long as the work in
question is in the public domain. Modern writers have been
mining the Greek tragedies for years."

"This isn't about Greeks, it's about French people back
when they had coaches and everything. I *do* know some Greeks
if you think that's better. They were very nice but kind of
dumb. They liked Joanne better than me. But that was probably because of her tits."

"This French classic," Harvey said, speaking very
slowly, as if he were hoping that if he spoke slowly enough, by
the time he finished his sentence it would be eleven o'clock and
he could legitimately have his first drink of the day, "does it
have a name?"

"Sure," Cathy said. "It was one of the paperbacks I
bought at the airport. It's called Something-or-other in the
Bedroom, and it's by this really *kinky* Frenchman. Do you
know which one I mean?"

"I'm afraid so," Harvey said.

"You *don't* think it's a good idea?" She appeared crest-
fallen.

"It depends."

"On what?"

"On how you plan to handle it."

"Well . . ." Cathy said. She could see that Harvey was
in some sort of pain. And it was important to have him in as
receptive a mood as possible. And anyway it *was* almost
eleven.

"Veronica X!" she called. Veronica X, who had been
floating lazily on an inflated raft in the middle of the pool,
looked up.

"Yassum?"

"It's almost eleven. Could you fix Mr. Bernstein a Bloody Mary?"

"Yassum!"

"And you might as well make me one too."

"Yassum!"

She (Veronica X) pulled herself languidly out of the sky-blue eighty-degree water.

"Y'all want 'em with celery salt?"

"Veronica X!" Harvey said sternly.

"Suh?"

"Will you for Christ's sake knock off that Uncle Tom crap and just go in there and make the goddamned Bloody Marys?"

"Certainly, Mr. Bernstein."

"And as a personal favor to me, would you try not to drip on the floor. It gets Ken all upset."

"You know something, Mr. Bernstein?" Veronica X said, slipping off her bikini, carefully wringing it out, and then putting it back on again. "It's sure God nice to have a man around the house."

"I think Veronica X has kind of a crush on you," Cathy said after Veronica X had gone. "I can't understand it, the terrible way you talk to her."

"It's all a matter of whether or not you were brought up with servants," Harvey said. "If you were, you know instinctively how to get along with them. It is not something that can be learned later in life."

"Anyway," Cathy said.

"Anyway?"

"My idea was this. Gregory Peck . . ."

"*Gregory Peck?*"

"You know what I mean. If you just say who could play the part, then you don't have to write all that dumb description. I mean, everybody *knows* what Gregory Peck looks like, right?"

"I suppose so. But what of posterity?"

"What?"

"What of the still unborn generations who might buy your book in some airport of the future? *They* may not know what Gregory Peck looks like."

"They can always see his old pictures on television."

"I never thought of that," Harvey said. Which was true. He hadn't. "Anyway, Gregory Peck . . . ?"

"Well, maybe Gregory Peck has made a million dollars being President Kennedy's dentist. We can either describe how he does it, or maybe President Kennedy just leaves it to him. You know, some kind of a will or something. *And to my faithful dentist, Gregory Peck, I leave* . . . Anyway, Gregory Peck is this big swinger and he's very worried about his daughter Jane Fonda who has been going to this fancy finishing school in the East. So he sends her out to the Coast to spend her summer vacation with his ex-mistress so she can learn about the Facts of Life. . . . Of course the way it's written now, it's pretty old-fashioned. They didn't have the pill then or electric toothbrushes, but . . ."

Harvey began to laugh.

"I don't see what's so funny," Cathy said.

"De Sade's *Philosophy in the Bedroom,* updated and set in Beverly Hills! An idea worthy of Max Wilk, Ed Hotchner, Max Shulman, or Christ knows how many Best-Selling assholes!"

"I've been meaning to ask you," Cathy said. *"Does* asshole have a hyphen or *doesn't* it? You keep changing your mind."

He was saved from answering this literary imponderable by the arrival of Veronica X and the Bloody Marys.

*   *   *   *   *

It was on this particular morning that the Studio common stock dropped another nine points on the big board and Smiling Jack conceived the notion of selling off the Studio's warehouses full of props, costumes, stagecoaches, riverboats, cannons, brassieres, fighter aircraft, and a few of the more presentable members of the New Talent School at public auction. Thus moving the unsuspecting Harvey Bernstein one step closer toward his inevitable fate.

Chapter TEN

1

The pink Mustang convertible, with its top down and the long blond hair of its driver streaming in its wake, roared past the corner where the old lady in the straw hat sells "Movie Star Maps" and with a screech of brakes swerved left off Sunset onto Carolwood Drive.

At the wheel, Jane Fonda, naked except for yellow-tinted sunglases, felt her heart beat faster! The soft Santa Ana wind caressed her nipples. . . .

*   *   *   *   *

"Cathy . . ."

"Mmmmmm?"

"*Nobody* is going to believe that Jane Fonda—and, by the way, you just *can't* use real people's names in a work of fiction—would be driving naked in a Mustang convertible on Sunset Boulevard in broad daylight."

"Why not?"

"Well, for one thing, she would be arrested."

"She drove a *space ship* stark naked in *Barbarella* and nobody arrested her."

"That was a *movie!* That was make-believe!"

"This is a *novel! It's* make-believe!"

It was their first quarrel. Cathy found it wildly exciting.

"You're supposed to be so *smart,* but you just don't know *anything!* Nobody *looks* at anybody else! Nobody *listens* to anybody else! Nobody gives a shit!"

With which she tore off her clothes, flung herself into *their* open-topped convertible Mustang (racing green), and gunned it down the driveway, turning south on Carolwood, heading toward Sunset.

She returned forty minutes later with a one-pound jar of fresh Iranian caviar and a magnum of champagne which she claimed she had bought at Jurgensen's in Beverly Hills.

"But you had no money."

"I opened a charge account."

"You had no identification."

"What about the birthmark on my ass?"

Harvey looked blank. Cathy burst into tears and fled into the house.

She *did* have a birthmark. Harvey was shocked to discover that he had never noticed it before. In her own way, Cathy was right. Nobody looks at anybody else. Nobody listens to anybody else. Nobody gives a shit.

*   *   *   *   *

He found her sobbing, cross-legged on the bed, struggling to open the bottle. As he attempted to yank it from her hands, the cork exploded, drenching them both.

Those readers who have never quarreled and then made love while splashing around in a bedful of Moët et Chandon would do well to re-examine the manner in which they are frittering away their lives.

2

That summer the phrase *life-style* was very much in fashion. It would soon (Harvey hoped) go the way of *with it, where it's at,* and *mother-grabbing,* but meanwhile there it was and it had to be dealt with.

"The life-style of a household," Harvey was explaining to Veronica X, "is almost always determined by its most nearly psychotic member."

They were seated by the pool. Harvey was working in a desultory fashion on Cathy's manuscript. Veronica X was thumbing through a Frederick's of Hollywood catalogue. Frederick's of Hollywood was a mail-order house specializing in G-strings, black lace see-through underwear, and boots with nine-inch spike heels. Its custom was drawn largely from professional strippers, Midwestern wives of the men of the silent majority, and Veronica X.

Veronica X had just borrowed Harvey's felt-tip pen to mark a pair of black mesh panties that featured a breakaway crotch and retailed at $3.95 when the racist aspect of Frederick's of Hollywood struck her with some force.

"How come no *white* lace underpants?" Veronica X said ominously. "The Black Man got no right to be turned on? That what they saying?"

It was conversations of this sort that had prompted Harvey's original remark.

"It is no easy thing," Harvey said, "to determine which member of our little household is the most nearly psychotic. Listen, Veronica X, do you really pee in the pool?"

"Every chance I get. The thing is, I have this water retention problem. But, man, we got to protest any way we can, right?"

She adored Harvey and regarded him as a kind of guru.

"Felix, he after me to marry him," Veronica X said presently.

Harvey took back his pen and pretended to busy himself with the manuscript. But Veronica X was not to be put off.

"Little fucker, he richer than God!" she said. "Little fucker claim he one hundred and *seven* years old, so what I got to lose?"

"The little fucker," Harvey said, "exaggerates shamelessly about everything. Perhaps he is also exaggerating about both his age and his total net worth. Besides," he said, trying to bring the conversation to a close, "he is of a different race."

"Little fucker richer than God," Veronica X said dreamily. "Little fucker buy Benguet Gold five cents a share. Ten thousand dollars' worth! Two hundred thousand shares. Little fucker, he got a ticker-tape machine in his bedroom. Benguet Gold closed yesterday at thirteen and seven-eighths."

Harvey continued to pretend to fuss with the manuscript.

"Mr. Bernstein?"

"Yes?"

"You ever eat something called salmon *mousse?*"

"Not when I can avoid it," Harvey said. "Listen, Veronica X . . ."

"Sir?"

"It's almost eleven. Will you fix me a Bloody Mary?"

"Certainly."

"Thank you."

"Only I took a water pill this morning. You don't mind if I pee first?"

"Christ, no. But make it snappy."

"Okay. Okay," Veronica X said. "Just in the shallow end."

*   *   *   *   *

Cathy had (wisely, Harvey thought) elected to go for the thick *in*sensitive novel.

He took one look at her and got this big fat hard-on!
A series of deft strokes with the felt-tip pen changed

this to, "He took one look at her and the crotch of his jeans bulged provocatively."

Follow Jane Fonda!

Follow that Mustang!

Follow this thick insensitive novel, if you can. . . .

Which was exactly what Harvey was trying to do.

It (the pink Mustang—Jane Fonda is also pink) turns into a driveway that winds through an acre or two of Technicolor lawn toward the mansion itself.

Juan Rodriguiz, the gardener's son, a lean twenty-three-year-old Aztec god, stripped to the waist, the color of burnished copper and glistening with sweat, brings his power lawn mower to a stop. (He was to be played by Jean Paul Belmondo.) He watches now as Jane alights from the Mustang. His eyes grow smoky with lust.

The crotch of his jeans (as previously mentioned) bulges provocatively.

Jane's arrival does not go unnoticed.

Nor does Belmondo's bulge.

Peeping through the dining-room window, the owner of the Mansion (Jeanne Moreau) and her younger brother (Dustin Hoffman) nod approval.

"Get a load of the wang on Juan," says Jeanne.

But Brother Dustin's eyes are riveted on the golden promise of Jane's throbbing . . .

* * * * *

Harvey Bernstein put down the manuscript and tasted the Bloody Mary. His third and it was still not twelve o'clock. Veronica X watched him like a Jewish mother anxiously awaiting the verdict on a plate of chicken soup.

"No celery salt," Harvey said, wanting her to know that he knew how much she cared.

"Little fucker hide the celery salt," she said cryptically.

Harvey did not wish to become involved in these below-stairs problems. Fat chance.

"You copee joint, I givee celery salt," Veronica X said in what Harvey presumed to be her imitation of Felix's imitation of how he thought she thought a Filipino should speak. Actually, they both spoke flawless English when they wanted to. Which was almost never. Role-playing had become a big part of their lives.

"My grandmother was a slave," Veronica X said. Her tone of voice suggested to Harvey's practiced ear that she was about to launch into an extended exercise in pseudo-autobiography. "I have a memory, kind of a race-memory, of the tourist-class deck of the slave ship. Chains. I remember the chains. Clank. Clank. Clank. And no place to pee. My grandmother had taken a water pill that morning. The morning she was seized by the white fuckers on the African shore. It was *our* Malibu," she added. "Marvelous little cottages, beach shacks, actually, but with excellent posters of some of the more interesting post-impressionists on the walls . . ."

It is important to explain that, at this point in his life, Harvey no longer listened to the actual *words* that persons addressing him were speaking, but rewrote automatically (in simultaneous translation) anything that was being said to him, generally improving the *quality* of the dialogue but distorting, perhaps, the literal meaning of the sounds that almost continuously vibrated against his eardrums.

In the bedroom, Cathy was typing the words:

The End

She would not tell Harvey until after lunch. It would give them something to celebrate.

PROLOGUE

(CONTINUED)

This is a suicide note.

I am, for once, totally alone. I will explain in a moment. But if I am ever to act, the time has come.

And my course is clear.

I must take this opportunity to set fire to the house, burning it (hopefully) to the ground.

I can think of no other way of gracefully disposing of my beloved's manuscript.

On the desk in Miss Thuringer's office are six neatly typed copies of "BEDROOM," a thick insensitive novel by Cathy Lewis Lovibond Lombard Lamont (Choose One).

I wonder what her real name is. I honestly believe she herself has forgotten.

The "novel" is indescribable.

I will not say that it is unpublishable. Apparently today *anything* is publishable.

I have considered the vanity presses. But I don't think that's the answer. Cathy is too smart. How in God's name did she ever hear of Homer Smith and the Yorkshire Press, who, she has decided, is to have the honor of presenting her prose to the pulsating American public? I am only grateful that she has not settled upon Alfred Knopf or Bennett Cerf.

It would be nice to think that after a quarter of a century toiling in the literary vineyards I still had some credit left. But I fear that that is not the case.

My three novels and two volumes of poetry (bearing the imprint of five different publishers) were dismal failures. My four hundred unfavorable book reviews have made me four hundred enemies. Eight hundred, if you count the wives, who always take these things more seriously.

I could, I suppose, call Barney at Grove Press.

We used to meet occasionally (Barney and I) at toy cocktail parties given at toy restaurants (e.g., The Four Seasons) to launch toy books by toy authors. My name was eventually stricken from even such lowly free lists when it was discovered that my influence was nil or was at least far out of proportion to my martini consumption. At such parties they used even to count the number of canapes. Not that I ever sinned in that direction.

But it was with Barney in mind that I conceived the dust-jacket photograph.

Which is why I am here alone today, drinking only moderately (for me) and plotting arson.

It was my vision (and one, I must say, excitedly agreed to by the other members of the household) that the jacket of "BEDROOM" be adorned with a photograph of its author (draped provocatively across an ornate Louis XVI bed) nude save for sunglasses and a quill pen.

There is no doubt that I am Lord and Master here. But I cannot help feeling that I am also, in a subtle way, the captive of my savage subjects. I cannot, for example, get *any* of them (except Felix) to wear clothes and have for the most part given up wearing them myself.

Now I think I *will* have a drink.

*   *   *   *   *

Since Felix and Veronica X have announced their engagement, domestic efficiency has increased one hundred per cent. At least there is ice in the ice bucket twenty-four hours a day.

And the cuisine is, I must say, superb. I, who have always been painfully thin, have begun to put on a little weight.

*   *   *   *   *

For the past week there has been high excitement about "The Auction." It appears that one of the major film studios is (for what appear to me to be obvious reasons) in dire financial straits and is, this very afternoon, selling off various properties that have been used over the years in its horrendous productions. A photograph of exactly the Louis XVI bed that we require for the jacket appeared two days ago in the Los Angeles *Times*.

My savage subjects have gone off in a body to see to its purchase. In addition, it is Veronica X's hope to obtain her trousseau from among such costumes as are left from a production called *Gold Diggers of 1933,* which she recently saw on late-night television.

Felix, reeking of cologne, beaming with pride, sporting a diamond-studded tie clip (worn five inches under his chin) and literally bulging with hundred-dollar bills, is prepared to go the limit in outfitting his bride-to-be.

I think he is full of shit. I don't believe he's a *day* over eighty!

*   *   *   *   *

Now to the logistics of the matter.

How to burn the place down?

The conflagration must not *start* in Miss Thuringer's office. That would be too obvious. And yet, the manuscript (all six copies of it) must not escape unscathed.

Perhaps if I soaked the living-room drapes in vodka and then applied a match . . .

It seems a fearful waste. But certain sacrifices must be made on the altar of art.

I will have another drink and consider the matter.

Chapter ELEVEN

1

Sound Stages Eight, Nine, Ten, and Eleven had been thrown together, leaving an open area large enough to contain (as they at one time or another had) the Sistine Chapel, the entire campus of "Midwestern University," where Jack Oakie used to go to school and Grady Sutton was perpetually a freshman, the stage of the Winter Garden Theater, the beach at Iwo Jima, Maxim's in Paris, the frozen fjords of Norway, the Emperor Nero's house seats at the Colosseum, the ruins of Trafalgar Square after the invasion of the Martians, and Dracula's castle.

Everyone was dressed to the nines.

Felix smelled so good that Veronica X was almost out of her mind.

All Hollywood was there. It took hell's own time to bring the multitudes into some kind of order.

The chief auctioneer of New York's Parke-Bernet had been flown in to handle the technical details. Smiling Jack hovered, smiling warmly. The public-address system, naturally, did not work immediately.

Ken had in his pocket twenty-five dollars with which he hoped to purchase *anything,* anything at *all,* that had once been worn by or in any way come in contact *with* the person of the late Judy Garland.

Cathy found the bed and stretched out on it. It was going to be just perfect. Harvey the Wise had been right again! Homer Smith would love it!

Tracy Steele arrived, outwardly calm but with crazed eyes.

There is something about an auction that turns everybody on.

They finally got the public-address system working.

Blah! Blah! Blah!

Some unnamed person bought a group of fourteen Roman chariots, sold as a lot.

There was a polite round of applause.

Two Mississippi River steamboats went.

Applause.

Edy Williams, a contract player, went, after spirited bidding, for twenty thousand dollars. It was meant to be a joke, a gag invented by the Head of West Coast Publicity, to get bidding off to a merry start. Both Edy and the buyer, however, took it all quite seriously.

He, a dark-haired Arabian oil millionaire, carried her off amid the popping of flash bulbs, deposited her in the back of his white Cadillac limousine, and drove away. Neither has been heard from since.

Felix bid and lost on a "merry widow" that had once cinched the waist of Betty Grable. He had had no intention of winning. He just wanted to see what the action was.

Some more stuff went.

And some more.

Sporadic applause.

Then more stuff.

Tracy Steele took a fast belt from his pocket flask, rose from the last row of the Abbey Rent's chairs that had been set up in the VIP section, and shouted, "Bull shit! I bid one million dollars for the whole goddamned studio!"

Veronica X nudged Felix and whispered, "That there Tracy Steele! That white fucker got *class!* He don't fuck around with no Shirley Temple's under*pants!*"

Felix raised his hand.

"Two million," he said.

"Three million," Tracy said. He was just playing around. But not really. His People had figured out to the penny exactly what it would cost to buy the studio. So much in cash and the rest in bank loans, using the studio itself, its real estate, film library, etc., as collateral. With its existing capital losses (huge for the current year) and its Canadian film-rental deductions it would be a pretty good buy for a man in Tracy's tax bracket, provided he was properly set up in a corporate way. Which he was.

"Four million," Felix said.

"Five," Tracy said.

"Six," Felix said.

Veronica X grabbed Cathy's arm. "Call Mr. Bernstein!" she whispered hoarsely. "Little fucker's gone ape-shit!"

"Seven," Tracy said.

"Seven-five," said Felix.

"Eight!" said Tracy.

"Eight-five!"

By this time the television cameras had moved into action. A microphone was shoved into Felix's face.

"Could you tell us, sir, for whom you are bidding?" the announcer asked.

"Little fucker just come to buy some underpants," Veronica X said.

"I am backed," Felix said with enormous dignity, "by substantial Philippine gold interests, and a short position in American Telephone and Telegraph."

Veronica X was suddenly caught up by the excitement of it all. "Don't forget about Ex-Lax!" she said.

"The lady is referring to the Xerox Company," Felix said, "but I assure you they are only involved in an unofficial way."

"Ten million!" Tracy shouted, trying desperately to get the television cameras back on him.

"This is becoming a bore," Felix said. "We are having *noisette de veau* for dinner and I must get home to prepare the sauce. Twenty million."

Cathy, working her way through the crowds, finally reached Tracy Steele's side.

"Jesus," Tracy said softly. "The lady with the gun!"

"Exactly," Cathy said.

"You got any *more* bright ideas for me?"

"The bid is to you, Mr. Steele," the auctioneer boomed. "Twenty million to you, sir?"

"Forty million!" Tracy said.

"Forty million! Forty million! Mr. Tracy Steele has just bid forty million!"

Pandemonium.

"What do you think we can actually buy this thing for?" Cathy said quietly.

"About a hundred."

"Do you have a hundred?"

"No. My People authorized me to go to fifty. Ten per cent in cash. The rest we can bank."

"Forty-*five*," Felix called from the other side of the sound stage. Veronica X was jumping up and down with excitement.

"Who's that squinty-eyed little bastard bidding against me?" Tracy asked.

"My cook," Cathy said. "I think this is just ridiculous. Why don't you join forces?"

"Your *cook?*" Tracy said.

"You should taste his salmon mousse," Cathy said.

"Salmon mousse is absolutely tasteless," Tracy said.

"I know," Cathy said. "I often wonder why he makes it."

"Does he *have* five million? In *cash?*"

"He'd probably have to sell some stock."

Smiling Jack wandered amiably onto the stage, smiled warmly at the audience, crinkled his nose boyishly at the auctioneer and hit him a sharp, low right to the gut, causing him to crumble to the floor.

"Speaking on behalf of the Studio," Smiling Jack said, "we bid sixty million."

"Seventy!" Cathy said.

"Eighty," Jack said, and without missing a beat, stepped into the role of the fallen auctioneer. "Eighty! Eighty! Eighty! Going once, going twice—"

"Ninety!" Cathy shouted.

"Have that woman removed," Jack said sweetly to a group of Studio guards.

"Ninety-two-five," Felix said.

"Ninety-*five*," Smiling Jack said. "And have that gook thrown out of here too."

"One *hundred* million!" Cathy said.

Smiling Jack's People were as smart as Tracy Steele's People. In fact they were the same People. One hundred was top dollar but still the right price. The sale of the Studio would obviously cause the shares to bounce up fifteen, maybe twenty points. Smiling Jack thought of his stock options. He thought of his five-year contract that would have to be bought off. He thought of his share in the pension and profit-sharing plan. He reached down, took Cathy by the hand, and helped her onto the improvised stage. His wide blue eyes like double shafts of sunlight through a stained-glass window at

St. Paul's Cathedral bathed her in an almost holy light.

"Lady," he said, "you just bought yourself a movie studio."

"In that case," Cathy said, "I would like the Marie Antoinette bed and whatever costumes you have from *Gold Diggers of 1933* packed and shipped to 1018 North Carolwood Drive. Delivery to be no later than five o'clock this afternoon."

Tracy Steele whispered something in Cathy's ear.

"One more thing," Cathy said to Smiling Jack. "Mr. Steele would like you to locate someone called Tiger Wilson and have him bring Mr. Steele's Ferrari around to what used to be your office. Where, by the way, we are all going for a quick drink to celebrate." She could not wait to call Harvey and tell him the good news.

"Veronica X!" she called from the platform. "Would you mind just asking Ken to scoot into Beverly Hills—I'm sure we'll need tomato juice."

Tracy's People and Smiling Jack's People (a genius named Lazar) was already in the office working out the details among himself. Cathy tried to call Harvey, but for some reason there was no answer.

Felix had no People, but after a quick phone call to ascertain the validity of his stock holdings Lazar agreed to deal for him too. He was very generous about the percentage. Normally business managers in situations such as this take twenty per cent. Lazar settled for a modest ten.

Ken arrived with the tomato juice.

There were many photographs and statements.

A press conference was called for the following morning.

It was almost six by the time they all got home.

The fire engines were still there. The cases containing the Marie Antoinette bed and the *Gold Diggers* costumes had been delivered and had been placed safely on the lawn.

The rest of the house (to the ultimate joy of Household Word and, conversely, to the despair of his insurance company) was a smoldering ruin.

The only surviving items were Harvey Bernstein, who was asleep (passed out) on the inflated raft in the middle of the pool, the palm trees (which had so wisely been fireproofed), and the original manuscript of "BEDROOM," a thick insensitive novel which Cathy Lewis Lovibond Lombard Lamont guarded at all times and which was lying safely in the oversize handbag she had taken with her to the Studio auction.

Chapter T W E L V E

1

The press conference had been called for eleven.

The new owners of the Studio met at ten.

"I suppose we'll have to elect officers and everything," Tracy Steele said sadly. Although he was head of a number of corporations, this kind of thing bored him. He usually let his People handle it.

"Instead of wasting a lot of time," Cathy said, "why doesn't everyone just write down on a piece of paper what he'd like to be?"

The results of the first ballot were as follows:

TRACY STEELE: President

FELIX: Chairman of the Board

HARVEY BERNSTEIN: Dead

The ladies had politely abstained from voting, and Ken could not figure out what he wanted to be. He was perfectly happy being a Best Friend.

"We've really got to find something for Harvey to do," Cathy said.

"He could be Head of the Studio," Tracy suggested. "He kind of *looks* like the Head of a Studio."

Harvey was dubious.

"What does the Head of a Studio have to *do?*" he asked.

"That," Tracy Steele said, "no one has ever been able to figure out."

"Well, okay then," Harvey said.

Wires and cables of congratulations had been pouring in, as is customary when a new power group takes over. Miss Thuringer, stationed at her new post, guarding the portals of the executive suite, was busy sorting them into different stacks.

The Catering Department had, as was *its* custom, sent up box lunches. The Chairman of the Board (Felix) sent them back untasted. He clutched Veronica X's hand and leaned toward her. (The smell of his cologne was so intoxicating that it became necessary for her to swallow several times rapidly in order to contain herself. Power in the male, even without the use of cologne, frequently produces similar reactions in those females still, happily, nonliberated). He whispered his instructions.

"The Chairman of the Board asks if Ken will please go to Jurgensen's and buy champagne and caviar," Veronica X said. "He further suggests that the Head of the Studio will probably require more tomato juice."

Ken was off like a shot.

He'd been going to Jurgensen's for tomato juice for years, but this was the first time he'd ever been sent by *The Head of the Studio!* He was, he felt, at last coming up in the world.

The former (although he did not yet know it) Head of West Coast Publicity wandered into the room unannounced.

"There are a hundred and fifty press people waiting outside, but not to worry," he said, smiling. "I've got your news release all written. It has to do with the studio's *life-style. A vital, youth*-oriented new management and all that crap . . ."

"Did I understand you to use the phrase *life-style?*"
Harvey said. He had been rummaging around the office looking for the bar. It was simply a matter of pressing a button
causing the bookshelves to slide back. Normally, he would have
found it in a trice. But he was far from well.

"Sure. *Life-style.* That's what the kids dig now."

Harvey turned to Cathy.

"Is it true that I am now—what was the title?—Head
of the Studio?"

"Of course, darling!"

"I do not wish to have in my employ anyone who uses
the phrase *life-style.*"

"Then fire him," Tracy said.

"You're fired," Harvey said.

He had found the button. The complete *Works of
Thackeray* slid away (left to right), revealing the bar. It even
had tomato juice. "Felix," Harvey said, "you are the Chairman
of the Board of this ridiculous Studio. Why is the ice bucket
empty?"

There was a knock at the door.

Harvey looked up. There were buttons to push which
dealt with the doors, but he had not as yet figured out how to
work them.

Miss Thuringer gingerly opened the door and poked her
head around it.

"Excuse me, Mr. Bernstein," she said. "There is a
gentleman here named Mr. Wilson. He thought you might be
needing ice."

"Show him in," Trace said.

Tiger entered, staggering under a two-hundred-pound
plastic bag of ice cubes.

"Hi, Trace."

"Hi, Tiger."

"Where would you like me to put these?"

"In my Bloody Mary," Harvey Bernstein said.

"The press is waiting," Cathy said. "We should probably have something to tell them."

They all thought for a moment.

"The Studio's first major motion picture," Cathy said, starting slowly, trying it on for size, "will be Harvey Bernstein's production, starring Tracy Steele, of 'BEDROOM,' my Best-Selling Novel soon to be published by Homer Smith, the President and founder of the Yorkshire Press.'

"Stop it!" Veronica X said, slapping away the Chairman of the Board's hand. "Later we copee jointee. Now we talkee pressee."

And out they went, to meet the cameramen and reporters.

2

That distinguished (and slightly batty) book publisher, Mr. Homer Smith, was mildly interested and even slightly pleased to read the small item in the morning paper announcing that a novel by one of his authors was to be made into a "major" motion picture. He had no idea in what way a "major" motion picture differed from any other sort of motion picture. In fact, he almost never went to the movies.

On a recent trip to Europe he had dined with Mr. Charles Chaplin (the dinner had been fair, the wines excellent). Greta Garbo had been at the house for tea on several occasions and had proved to be far more talkative and outgoing than her public reputation for shyness and silence would have suggested. It had been, in the end, rather difficult to shut her up. And that, as far as his knowledge of the cinema went, was about the size of it.

Being a man of fastidious politeness, he had handed the newspaper (after he had finished the crossword puzzle) to his secretary, asked her to dispatch a telegram of congratulations to "that girl, whatever her name is," and promptly dismissed the matter from his mind.

3

As the Studio was practically deserted (except for the key technicians who, by union regulations, arrived each morning at eight and left at six whether there was anything in production or not), it seemed sensible to Cathy that the group take up temporary residence there.

Cathy and Harvey found "Star Bungalow A" even more comfortable than their quarters at what had, until yesterday, been 1018 North Carolwood Drive.

Tracy Steele moved back into his twelve-room suite in the Emmenthal Building. The members of the New Talent School were relocated without incident (by Tiger Wilson) into the Petit Trianon or at least into a lavishly constructed replica that had been standing vacant for some years on the back lot. The lack of bathing facilities (the only detail that had been omitted) did not seem to bother them at all.

The tank on Stage Five (where the Battle of Trafalgar had been so triumphantly won—who will ever forget Mickey Rooney in *Kiss Me Hardy?* Certainly not the stockholders. It *had* seemed like a good idea at the time. Mr. Rooney had had, earlier in his career, the advantage of starring in a hugely successful series bearing an extraordinarily similar title) was converted into an extremely workable swimming pool. Ken saw to it that it was kept at a constant temperature of eighty degrees.

As an economy measure the commissary was closed down, but the Chairman of the Board, assisted by the newly appointed Vice-President in Charge of Black Relations, took personal charge of the Executive Dining Room. The quality of the food improved immeasurably.

Harvey was delighted. Perhaps Cathy's attention could

be diverted from the publication of her novel to its direct trans-ference to the screen. This, it appeared to him, would save everyone concerned a great deal of embarrassment.

*   *   *   *   *

Lacking anything better to do, Harvey wandered down to a building called "The Still Gallery," where the Louis XVI bed had been set up and Cathy (with a full complement of hairdressers, body-makeup people, and a Master of Properties) was posing for the dust-jacket cover.

Harvey's appearance in the gallery caused an uncommon stir. It is not often that a Studio Head and a camera (even a still-camera) are seen in the same room. "All right, children," the director said. "Let's take ten!"

The director was young and kind of groovy-looking. Since his *Anna Karenina* project had been so abruptly canceled, he was grabbing what work he could. Cathy had decided he would be ideal to direct the jacket cover. His People (Lazar) had talked him into taking the assignment. "What the hell, kid, a day's work is a day's work. You do a good job, maybe I can get you a shot at the picture."

Cathy was in a state of high excitement.

"Darling," Cathy said to Harvey, "I hate to bother you with details like this, but André thinks there's something wrong with the sunglasses."

"The quill pen is sensational, Harve," the director said (they had not yet been formally introduced), "and I only wish to Christ I'd thought of it myself. But the sunglasses. I don't seem to *feel* them. I mean, I don't think they even *had* them in those days. I mean, like, you never see them in period pictures."

"Sweetheart," Harvey said (he was getting the idea rapidly), "the story takes *place* in the past but it was written in the *present*."

"You mean you want to get the feeling of two different time periods in the same shot?"

"I mean I want her to be wearing sunglasses and holding a quill pen."

The Master of Properties appeared at his side with a large coffee mug.

"Sorry about the celery salt, Mr. Bernstein," he said. "And I didn't know how you felt about Tabasco."

"No Tabasco," Harvey said.

"Right, sir," the Master of Properties said. "Next time I'll know."

(As anyone who has ever been connected with the manufacture of a motion picture will tell you, it may take a certain minor talent to write, direct, produce, or star in a movie, but it takes *genius* to be a good propman.)

"In other words," the director said, "what you'd like to get is an almost Fellini-esque sense of *time* and *non*-time?"

"I want her wearing sunglasses and holding a quill pen."

"Jesus!" the director said. He suddenly felt very young and very small, both of which he was. "I don't know if I can bring it off, but, by God, I'll try!"

"And also maybe you could do something about her *hair*."

"Of course! You don't have to *tell* me what you want, but if you could somehow give me an *indication*."

"If you could get it combed out of her eyes so we could see her face."

"You mean sort of *back*? So we can see more of her *face?*"

"Something like that."

"Jesus, Harve," the director said. "You know, this is *exciting!* It'll take a couple of minutes to relight, of course."

Harvey and the Master of Properties exchanged glances. Miraculously, the second coffee mug contained exactly the right amount of celery salt and all traces of Tabasco had vanished. The mug switching, which occurred before the eyes of at least thirty people, was totally invisible.

"Listen," Harvey said. (They had stepped into her trailer which was air-conditioned and therefore required her to put on a robe.) "I don't know why we don't just forget about publishing the book. Why don't we make it directly as a movie?"

"I'd thought of that too," Cathy said. "But then I got this wire from Homer this morning."

"Homer who?" Harvey said with sinking heart.

"Isn't it Homer *whom?*" Cathy said and handed him the telegram.

It had been sent full-rate, addressed to Miss Cathy Lewis Lovibond Lombard Lamont, care of the Studio, and said:

DELIGHTED TO READ THAT A NOVEL TO BE PUBLISHED BY US IS BEING MADE INTO A QUOTE MAJOR UNQUOTE MOTION PICTURE. PERHAPS WHEN YOU ARE NEXT IN NEW YORK YOU MIGHT BE FREE TO JOIN US FOR TEA. MISS GARBO IS LONGING TO MEET YOU. MY SINCEREST CONGRATULATIONS AND BEST WISHES FOR THE SUCCESS OF OUR MUTUAL ENTERPRISE

HOMER SMITH

The "Miss Garbo" part had been added by the secretary who sent the wire. She happened to be an appalling name-dropper and frequently fantasized about being invited, on some quiet afternoon, to the boss's house to take tea with Miss Garbo.

Garbo's okay, but not that big a deal to meet socially.

Her main value is afterward. Being able to say, "I had tea with Garbo last week," still makes a lot of points in some circles.

"Isn't it exciting?" Cathy said. *"You're* going to make my movie and Mr. *Smith* is going to publish my book!"

The director tapped discreetly on the trailer door. "Ready when you are, H.B.," he said.

Cathy beamed at Harvey.

Her *lover!* Her *teacher!* The Head of Her *Studio!* The man who, without apparently doing *anything,* had made all this possible!

Cathy slipped out of her robe and went back to work.

Harvey went looking for the propman.

He did not have far to look.

"I think I've *really* got it right this time," the propman said. "You must remember, sir, it takes *any* studio a certain length of time to adjust to the requirements of a new regime."

Chapter THIRTEEN

1

The Screenwriter had been highly recommended by Lazar. "Most of what he writes is crap, but it's high-*class* crap, if you know what I mean," Lazar had said. "He also happens to be suing the Studio for two hundred and fifty thousand dollars, which puts us in a very strong bargaining position."

The logic of this escaped Harvey, but then much of Lazar's logic escapes most people. He is almost always right, though.

"Will he have to read the book?" Harvey asked nervously.

"Not necessarily. He won an Academy Award two years ago for"—he named one of the best-selling novels of the past ten years—"and I know damn well he didn't read *that.*"

This was a lie. The Screenwriter had *tried* to read the novel. It was just that he had never been able to *finish* it. As no one else had ever been able to finish it either, it made, in the end, no appreciable difference. His youngest son had taken the resulting Oscar to school as part of a "show and tell" thing and lost it, leaving it on the bus or somewhere.

He had won another one earlier on in his career which he had given to a girl while drunk one night for reasons that probably seemed very sound at the time but which he could no longer remember.

"He sounds ideal," Harvey said. "Is he very expensive?"

"Very. But don't worry about it. I'm sure I can work something out with his People."

* * * * *

They met in Harvey's office the following morning. The Screenwriter was a tall, melancholy man in his late forties. He wore army pants, a windbreaker, and black velvet slippers with large gold monograms on the toes.

He walked directly to the bookcase, pushed the correct button, and poured himself an enormous drink. "At least you've got ice," he said, dropping wearily onto the couch. "The last three sons of bitches who had this office, you could never get them to keep ice in the ice bucket. No wonder the Studio is on its ass."

Harvey was impressed.

Although it was only ten o'clock in the morning, Harvey did not think it was polite to allow his visitor to drink alone.

As is customary in such meetings, the *subject* of the meeting was avoided as long as possible. The Screenwriter spoke at considerable length of some minor difficulties he was having with his Rolls Royce.

Harvey spoke admiringly of the Screenwriter's slippers.

The Screenwriter explained that since Peal's (his London bootmaker) was now defunct, he had had to have them send his last to some jerk in Santa Monica whose prices were high but whose workmanship was inferior.

They both spoke, in sorrow, of the decline of craftsmanship in the world.

"Nobody gives a shit any more," the Screenwriter said. "No one seems to take any pride in his work."

He rose and refilled both their glasses.

He glanced at his watch and sighed. He had a lunch date at Hillcrest at twelve-thirty. It was impossible to stall any longer.

"This thing I'm supposed to write," he said. "Can you kind of just tell me the story or do I have to *read* it?"

This was the moment that Harvey, too, had been dreading.

"I don't know which is worse," Harvey said.

"It's not about Ireland, is it?" the Screenwriter asked hopefully. "In the days of the Trouble?"

"No," Harvey said.

"Good. There is nothing more depressing than two Jews sitting down together to discuss making a picture about Ireland during the days of the Trouble."

Harvey felt a sudden inexplicable surge of warmth toward this man. He blurted out the truth. "It's mostly about screwing," he said.

The Screenwriter nodded.

"East Coast or West Coast?"

"I beg your pardon?"

"The screwing," the Screenwriter said patiently. "Does it take place on the East Coast or the West Coast?"

"Does it matter?"

"Not really. I used to just write East Coast screwing. It was kind of a snob thing. Now I do both, so no strain either way."

"West Coast," Harvey said.

"Kids?" the Screenwriter asked.

"No kids."

The Screenwriter got up and fixed himself another drink. "A picture about grown-ups screwing other grown-ups?"

Harvey nodded.

"Jesus," the Screenwriter said, "if I'd known that I wouldn't have had my People be so tough on your People."

He was silent for a moment.

"I'll be goddamned," he said. "Maybe I *better* read this thing."

"The quality of the prose leaves something to be desired."

"Naturally. If it didn't why would you be paying me all that money?"

"To be quite frank about it," Harvey said, "our little tale is simply an ill-written version of De Sade's *Philosophy in the Bedroom,* brought up-to-date and set in Beverly Hills."

The Screenwriter rose and began to pace rapidly back and forth across the office. Something in the idea seemed to ignite his creative fires. "We call it 'Bedroom,' of course," he said thoughtfully. "And Greg Peck is this big swinger. He's worried about his daughter, Jane Fonda. She's been through the whole New England finishing school bit, but she's still a virgin. I don't know how we sell *that* exactly . . . but don't worry . . . that's *my* problem. Maybe a scene with—okay— Greg has sent her out to the Coast for her summer vacation. He has this ex-mistress, Deborah Kerr, and . . . shit! I can see the opening shot. Fade in. Ext. Sunset Boulevard. Day. A black convertible Mustang—"

"Pink," Harvey said.

"A *pink* convertible Mustang with its top down speeds toward the camera. Closer shot. We see that the driver is Jane Fonda. And she's *naked!*"

"Except for sunglasses," Harvey said.

"Except for sunglasses. Christ, what an opening! What do you think, Harve?"

"I don't think there's any reason in the world for you to read the book."

"Great," the Screenwriter said. "I usually work better that way anyhow."

∗ ∗ ∗ ∗ ∗

Lazar telephoned later from Hillcrest, where he had just finished lunch. "I heard you had a very good meeting?"

"Well," Harvey said, "he *did* seem to have an almost intuitive grasp of the material."

"I've never seen him so excited," Lazar said. "He thinks he can have a first draft screenplay for you in three weeks."

"That soon?" Harvey said in some dismay.

"He says there are great parts for Tracy and Jane and Greg and Deborah and Richard and Elizabeth. I've already been in touch with their People. . . ."

∗ ∗ ∗ ∗ ∗

Four weeks from the day of his meeting with Harvey, the Screenwriter delivered the script. He had finished it in three but, because of his high level of professional integrity, he would not have dreamed of violating the Writing Profession's Second Commandment: THOU SHALT NOT DELIVER THY MATERIAL LESS THAN ONE WEEK LATE. (The First Commandment being: THOU SHALT NOT, UNDER ANY CIRCUMSTANCES, GIVE BACK THE MONEY. The other eight are of less importance, having to do with working at home rather than at the Studio, the bust measurements of Studio-assigned secretaries, reimbursement for alcohol actually *consumed* while on the job, participation in the cassette rights, and kindred matters.)

He tossed the bound manuscript casually onto Harvey's desk and headed for the bar.

"Of course, this is just a rough," he said.

(Seventh Commandment: THOU SHALT NEVER

ADMIT THAT THOU HAST WORKED THY BRAINS
OUT ON SOMETHING AND THINK IT IS ABSO-
LUTELY SENSATIONAL.)

He had, in truth, been dictating eighteen hours a day
to a battery of three secretaries (44–24–44, 43–20–36, and
20–38–48—the one who could type). He had polished the
screenplay with loving care and caused it to be multilithed
in the necessary edition of one hundred and fifty copies.

His People had insisted on being paid by certified check
before the actual delivery. People have their own set of Commandments.

Harvey, who had never seen a movie script before,
weighed it carefully in his hand, trying to think of something
to say. He looked at the number of the last page: 125. "Is it
the right length?" he asked. Considering the fact that the
novel had run more than four hundred pages, it seemed very
short for so much money.

"It's about ten minutes long," the Screenwriter said.
"You always put in a certain amount of crap so the Director
can have something to cut out. It gives him the feeling he's
making a *contribution*."

(Director's Fourth Commandment: THOU SHALT
ALWAYS SAY, "OF COURSE, I HAD TO DO A LOT
OF WORK ON THE SCRIPT MYSELF.")

"But do you think it's"—Harvey groped for the word
—"all *right?*"

"You mean, will it play?"

"I guess so."

"Sure."

"But," Harvey said after a time, "how do we handle
the, you know, *screwing* parts?"

The Screenwriter seemed baffled by the question.

"That's essentially the Director's problem," he said.

"But I *imagine* you hire some actors, tell them to screw, and take a picture of it."

Although he had twenty-three screen credits (and two Academy Awards) he had never, as a matter of principle, set foot on a sound stage.

"But will they *do* it?"

"Will *who* do *what?*"

Until this moment he had found Harvey to be the most sensitive and intelligent Head of a Studio he had ever worked with. He could not understand this sudden breakdown of communication. Was Harvey trying to *tell* him something? Had the check not really been *certified?* Or was he just trying to ease him out of the cassette rights? He wondered if he ought to make some excuse to leave the room and telephone his People.

Harvey was sweating now and looked so goddamned *innocent* that the Screenwriter decided to play along.

"Would you mind repeating the question?" the Screenwriter said.

"Can you actually *get* actors to—well, *screw* on the screen?"

"Jesus!" the Screenwriter said. "A lot of them have it written into their contracts. The way the old-time stars used to write in the number of their close-ups. You can't get anyone who means a shit at the box office today who doesn't *insist* on at least a *couple* of screwing scenes. With *our* script"—(THOU SHALT ALWAYS USE THE PHRASE *OUR SCRIPT*, THUS IRREVOCABLY LOCKING THE PRODUCER INTO ANY FUCK-UP THAT MIGHT AND PROBABLY WILL OCCUR LATER)—"you got no problems castingwise. The whole damn thing is *nothing* but screwing. In one scene, in reel five I think it is, even the *butler* gets to throw Jane a little bang."

"The last movie I saw," Harvey Bernstein said, "was *Alexander's Ragtime Band* with Tyrone Power, Don Ameche, and Alice Faye. Did you ever know Alice Faye? *In person,* I mean?"

The Screenwriter nodded.

"Tell me about her," Harvey said.

The Screenwriter relaxed. There was no need to call his People. Everything was going to be okay.

"Why don't we have another drink?" he said.

"There was a picture," Harvey said, "where she wore this funny little sailor hat. It was with Dick Powell, I think. . . ."

2

"What is a boom shot?" Cathy said. They were lying in bed. Cathy was reading the script. Harvey had already taken his pills.

"I have no idea," Harvey said.

"It doesn't matter. André says he never reads the script before he directs a picture. He says he works better that way."

* * * * *

Tracy Steele had always wanted to screw Jane Fonda. In the script he got to screw her a number of times.

"I love it, Harve," he said on the phone from the Springs the following day. "I. Mean. I. Really. Love. It. Let me put Frank on. He says he'd like to do the Gardener. Just as a Cameo thing. One day. No billing. Just expenses."

"And I'll do as many takes as you want," Frank said.

"Don't worry, Harve," Tracy said. "Frank's People are getting in touch with our People."

* * * * *

"What is a boom shot?" Elizabeth said. They were lying in bed. Elizabeth was reading the script. Richard had already taken his pills.

"I have no idea, luv," Richard said.

"It doesn't matter. At least somebody has sent us a script."

"What's it about?" Richard said sleepily.

"Screwing," Elizabeth said.

"Super," Richard said, smothering a yawn. "Why don't you have our People get in touch with their People in the morning?"

* * * * *

Harvey's People had sent out thirty copies of the script to thirty leading movie stars all of whom were over thirty. His phone did not stop ringing for a week.

The only turndown they got was Jane Fonda.

"It's not that I don't think it's a *darling* script," Jane said. "But it just doesn't seem, you know, like really *relevant*."

* * * * *

"Maybe I'll have to play the part myself," Cathy said.

PROLOGUE

(CONTINUED)

1

This is a suicide note.

This time I am serious.

The joke that my life has become (has always been, for that matter) is over.

There is tonight to get through; that much at least I owe to Cathy. She is looking forward to it so. "The single most transcending moment of my life," she says. As far as I can see, her life has been an almost unending series of single most transcending moments. May it ever be thus!

I have booked passage on a tramp steamer that leaves San Pedro at dawn tomorrow bound for Liverpool, via the Panama Canal, Curaçao, and God knows where. It does not matter. I shall not be long aboard.

When the time is ripe, perhaps the third night out, I shall totter, drunken and unafraid, to the rail and, in one last swan dive of despair (belly flop is, I fear, more my style) plunge silently overboard into the black velvet oblivion of the Pacific Ocean, which is kept (I am told) at a constant temperature of eighty degrees.

* * * * *

Miss Thuringer has placed a cup of instant coffee at my elbow. I have gone to the bar and made the necessary adjustments.

Ken has already left for the airport to meet Mr. Homer Smith.

His presence at tonight's festivities (if that is the word) was arranged by subterfuge.

Miss Garbo is to be presented with an "honorary" award and he has been persuaded to serve as her escort.

At least I like to think that he is motivated thus. Although the publicity value of his appearance cannot have escaped him. The "novel," publication date timed to coincide with the premiere of the film (December 24th, last), has been on the Best Seller list for eight weeks.

He (Mr. Smith) had, at least, the wisdom to decline the invitation to appear with his author on that (now famous) Johnny Carson Show. Poor Johnny! I met him briefly backstage just before air time. He seemed a gentle, kindly man, but he had not, unfortunately, got around to reading the book. I hear from him occasionally. Things are better now. He has found employment as a disc jockey on an Omaha radio station under a different name. (Omaha is not the city; I have been sworn to protect his anonymity.)

It was not his fault. Normally they tape these things in advance. But he had caught a nasty cold and so . . . "What the hell," he said, "it won't kill us to do the show *live* for once!"

That's what he thought. . . .

* * * * *

If only *my own life* could have been pre-taped! At least I would have had a chance to edit out . . . what? My wretched childhood? The Army? My marriage to Margery? My children whom I neither know nor understand? My time with Cathy?

When I consider how my life is taped . . .

I guess, probably, I would cut out everything but the commercials.

And a few glorious hours with Cathy. No, they could go too. Forty-seven years of pain cannot conceivably be redeemed by a few golden moments bouncing (however joyously) on kitchen floors and squishing ravenously on champagne-drenched beds. I have made my decision. The editing (The Final Cut, as I have been taught to call it in the semantic of my new profession) will occur three midnights hence on the softly rolling deck of the S.S. . . .

This is a suicide note.

* * * * *

I have, I must admit, met, during the past six months, a number of interesting people.

Greg is divine. Under other circumstances, we would, I choose to think, have become close friends. But the Head of the Studio must perforce remain to a certain degree aloof from his Players.

Frank is sensational. (His one-day bit as the Gardener has earned him a Best Supporting Nomination.) And true to his word, he was terribly generous about retakes, working, it turned out, far into the night.

Of Richard and Elizabeth I cannot speak too highly. Professional, charming, and on several occasions where the script was vague, highly inventive and original.

Although I am listed as Producer, I have not seen a foot of the film. Nor shall I ever.

The sight of my beloved, seventy feet wide, in the arms of ten or twelve of the most attractive leading men in the world would be more than I could bear.

I am told, however, by those who are in a position to know such things, that the opening sequence of Cathy in the pink convertible Mustang, shot on Sunset Boulevard one misty (smoggy) Sunday morning, is almost lyric in its poetic beauty.

I can well believe it.

Apparently the Ford Motor Company agrees. Having been shown the sequence, they have supplied us all, free of charge, with convertible Mustangs in colors of our choice. Mine is black with red leather upholstery and wire wheels.

The Screenwriter (his People were right—the crap he writes is of the highest possible quality) has devised a way around any censorship problems that might have arisen. The whole story now takes place in our heroine's mind: the erotic fantasies of a slightly repressed finishing-school graduate while traveling to California to spend the summer with her rather straitlaced maiden aunt. Deborah has been switched from Greg's ex-mistress to his unmarried sister.

This concept (when it struck him, the Screenwriter became so excited that he spilled his drink. He jumped up and down for a full minute in front of my desk shouting the incomprehensible phrase, "A dirty 8½! A dirty 8½!") has had innumerable advantages.

For one thing, it has permitted us to utilize to almost unnecessarily graphic advantage the host of "Guest Stars" who so merrily volunteered their services once they understood the nature of the project. "But what," says André, his dark brown eyes gleaming with excitement and stupidity, "could be more *natural?* Why *shouldn't* a schoolgirl use well-known film stars as the objects of her sexual daydreams?"

André has also "opened up" (as he calls it) the script.

I, like our heroine, choose to regard the forty days of shooting as a kind of fantasy of my own. It could not all really have happened!

The scene, for example, shot on location in the locker room of the Los Angeles Rams (a local football team) at the end of the Green Bay Packers game! It was what "we" call a "stolen shot." André posing as a TV cameraman with a hand-held Arriflex and Cathy in football garb (from Western Costume) made their way into the locker room. Both undressed (the Arriflex had been waterproofed) and were waiting as both the offensive and defensive teams joined them in the steaming shower. Once Cathy's presence was discovered, André (and his camera) was totally ignored. The resulting footage is said to be incredible.

Cathy (she reports) never had a better time.

That they both escaped with their lives is only a comment on today's general acceptance of naked girls and TV cameramen turning up in the damnedest places at the damnedest times.

$*$ $*$ $*$ $*$ $*$

Perhaps, since this is my ultimate and absolutely guaranteed final revised draft suicide note, I can indulge myself to the extent of including a few of my own production notes from a journal sporadically and disjointedly kept during the making of our film.

They (my notes) will explain far better than anything I could write this morning the state of mind that has brought me to this, my final farewell.

$*$ $*$ $*$ $*$ $*$

NOTES FROM HARVEY BERNSTEIN'S
PRODUCTION JOURNAL

Cathy's suggestion that she play the leading role herself has been taken with more seriousness than I could ever have imagined. I, in my role as Father-Figure, have insisted on a screen test. I do not know exactly what a screen test is. But surely she will fail it, never having been before a camera in her life.

* * * * *

I had forgotten! I had forgotten!

A furtive-looking individual named Gersten arrived at the studio this morning with six cans of film under his arm.

The Production Staff (my God, where did all these people spring from!), forty in all, hairdressers, costumiers, lighting cameramen, my friend the Master of Properties, André and his suddenly acquired assistants (he is now insisting on a Best Friend of his own—as if two Best Friends, Ken and Tiger, were not sufficient!), the Head of this and the Head of that were all assembled in Projection Room One at noon. Cathy and I sat in the back row, holding hands. "I want you to be completely honest, darling," she whispered as the lights went down, "completely *honest!* I don't want people to think I got the part just because I was the Producer's Girl Friend!"

The screen flickered.

Cathy gripped my hand. I could feel her tension.

"You've got to remember," she whispered, "the kind of equipment we were working with. We had to sneak everything, including the lights and the camera, into the motel in *suitcases!* And I'm sure the sound is just *terrible!*"

A young man dressed as a burglar ("That's Jigger. You remember, I wrote about him in Lessons Four through Six") enters the room and looks around. It is empty. He hears a sound and, his face registering something that I presume he intends to indicate panic, conceals himself in the closet. The door to the room opens again. Cathy is revealed in evening dress. She is fighting off the unwanted attentions of her escort (played, presumably for economic reasons, by the furtive Mr. Gersten). Finally, but not before he has managed to tear her evening dress sufficiently to reveal for a fleeting instant her glorious left bosom ("We got the dress at Frederick's! It's a breakaway. That and the motel room, of course, were the two biggest items on the budget!''), she manages to escape from his clutches, slam the door, and lock it in his face.

She looks around, obviously trying to locate the camera, and heaves an exaggerated sigh of relief.

"Thank God," she says, "I have managed to escape the clutches of that terrible man. Little did I know when I accepted his invitation to dine at Trader Vic's that the evening would end like this!"

She was right about the quality of the sound. She seemed to be speaking on the long-distance telephone from Spain.

She crosses to the mirror by the dressing table and (she has found the camera by now and is playing to it) slowly begins to remove her clothes.

A sudden hush falls over the projection room. Our forty technicians are hooked. The Master of Properties hands me my coffee mug. It is full of *coffee* and he is breathing hard. Good God!

Naked at last (it must be remembered that I have almost never seen her with her clothes on—but somehow up there on the shaky black-and-white screen the effect is totally different—almost *devastating*), she prepares for bed. The closet door opens. The burglar emerges and removes his mask.

("What a ham!" Cathy whispers. "Why would a burglar take off his *mask?* Now I'll be able to describe him to the police. But he just wanted to make sure the audience saw his face. I don't think he's all *that* good-looking, do you?")

He looks like a dim-witted beachboy, which, I imagine, he probably is. As a matter of fact, he looks a little like a more masculine Ken. André clearly has the same idea. "Not much of an actor," he says aloud, "but great Best Friend material!"

He is shushed vigorously by the rest of our little audience.

The burglar advances to the bed.

Cathy attempts to cover herself with a sheet. Savagely he rips it away.

"What do you want?" Cathy says from Spain on a bad connection.

"You know what I want," he says to the sound accompaniment of a number of pesetas being dropped into a pay phone in Valencia.

Then he too, favoring the camera, begins slowly to remove his clothes.

"Adorable!" Ken's voice from the darkness.

"Shhhhhhhh!" from the multitudes.

Cathy leaps from the bed. There is a chase around the room.

"Gersten said this was supposed to be the comedy relief," Cathy whispers. "But nobody's laughing."

No one was.

Finally he catches her and throws her to the bed. His organ rises. But imperceptibly.

"Much ado about nothing!" Ken says scornfully in darkness.

"It was the *third* take!" Cathy replies, rising loyally to her costar's defense.

"Shhhhhhhh!"

If the scene that followed proves anything at all, it proves that the act of sexual intercourse becomes more difficult, if not indeed impossible, when the two parties involved are concentrating their total attention on the camera. The burglar, approaching climax, pauses to adjust his cowlick. Surreptitiously he licks a finger and touches his camera-side eyebrow. Cathy rearranges her hair, spread out behind her on the pillow. (Actors, I later learn, during the course of our *real* production, are, for reasons unknown, almost passionately concerned about their hair to the exclusion of practically everything else.)

The film ends on a fairly repulsive close shot of the
burglar's face.

Total silence in the projection room. I have recently
come to know about silences. There are good silences. Bad
silences. And electric silences. This one, I later learn, is an
electric silence.

The second film (there are three) comes on almost at
once.

In the second film the young man wears a Nazi uniform. Cathy is a captured member of the French Under-
ground. (A photograph of de Gaulle hangs over the motel
bed. That is the only change in the setting.) He attempts to
extract her secrets by fair means or foul. This one has more of
a plot. Cathy turns the tables upon him. She becomes the
aggressor. "Encore!" "Encore!" "Encore!" she says from time
to time. Eventually her oppressor slumps to the floor, simu-
lating unconsciousness, and finally expires with a considerable
amount of deep breathing. Cathy, naked and triumphant,
reaches under the pillow and withdraws a tricolor. "Fuck the
Nazi devils!" she declaims in a slightly Southern accent. "Unto
the death if necessary! *Vive la France!*"

This time the projection room breaks into spontaneous
applause.

At the end of the third film, about the Butler and the
Maid, there is what can only be called a standing ovation.
Hollywood is full of so-called yes-men. But these bravos were,
to my ear at least, totally genuine.

"Do you think it went all right, darling?" Cathy said.
"Do you think they *liked* me?"

She knew perfectly well how it went. So did I. So did
everyone.

The lights went up.

André rose from his seat.

"Ladies and gentlemen," he said. "I think we here in

this room today have witnessed something rare and something beautiful, something that none of us, however long we shall continue to be associated with this great industry, will ever forget. Thus whoever it was must have felt when he first laid eyes on Lana seated demurely at the soda fountain at Schwab's Drugstore. Thus must that photographer, whatever his name was, who took the photograph of Marilyn have felt as her image came shimmering to his eyes through the developing fluid in his darkroom. Ladies and gentlemen. I feel very humble and at the same time very proud to have been present at the moment when . . . *a star is born!*"

*   *   *   *   *

This is a suicide note.

*   *   *   *   *

PRODUCTION NOTES CONTINUED

Cathy has become obsessed with her hair. We have hired, at great expense, a man named Sidney Something who is said to be a genius in the field. God knows he has done wonders with her hair. And, personally, he could not be more charming. His only drawback, socially, is that while each morning he shakes hands with Cathy in a formal fashion he insists on *kissing* me. At first I objected. Then I became resigned. Now I have come to enjoy and *expect* it. One day last week he failed to kiss me. I sulked throughout the morning feeling vaguely depressed without quite knowing why. I wandered down to the set. Sidney, too, was sulking in a corner. The action on the stage had come to a complete halt. Cathy had, uncharacteristically, locked herself in her trailer.

"What is it, Sidney?" I said. "What have I done?"

He declined to look up from his copy of *Women's Wear Daily.*

"Was it the *wig?*"

No answer. But I continued to press.

"Was it something I *said* about the wig?"

Trouble had been brewing for several days about the wig. I thought it made her look ridiculous. If someone has been swimming in a pool and emerges with her every hair in place, I *still* think it looks ridiculous.

Sidney refused to look up.

"It's made of genuine hair," he said, between clenched teeth. "*Nun's* hair, if you want to know! I worked on it for a week."

The entire set was silent. As I have mentioned before, there are different kinds of silences. This silence was Electric.

We were having, although I did not know it at the time, our first *showdown.*

The cast, the crew, the entire world, I suppose, was waiting to see who was *boss.*

A compromise must be reached. Neither party must lose face. I must emerge as *boss.* But Sidney's artistic freedom must not be curtailed.

"Sidney," I said. "I have an idea."

"I am *aware* of that. You have made yourself *perfectly* clear."

"Perhaps I expressed myself badly."

Out of the corner of my eye, I could see Cathy's trailer door open slightly and her head peek out.

André was at the other end of the stage shooting pool with Tracy. Felix (the Chairman of the Board) was off fixing lunch.

I was alone.

God (in Whom I do not believe but Who if He *does*

159

exist will doubtless turn out to be a Hairdresser) touched me
on the shoulder.

"Sidney," I said. "Why don't we shoot it both ways?"

"You mean shoot it *with* the wig and then again *without* the wig?"

"Something like that. Then *you* look at the film and *you*
decide which is better."

"Pussycat!" Sidney said, rising and kissing me full
upon the lips.

The stage came to life.

André, still carrying his pool cue, wandered back to
the battlefield. "All right, children," he said. "Why don't we
press on. I have two more setups to get before lunch!"

Cathy, followed by her body-makeup people, dashed
from her trailer and threw her arms around me. Getting, I
must add, pancake makeup all over my white bush jacket.

But it was worth it.

"You know what," Sidney said to Cathy. "I think
Harve's right. I think the hair *should* be wet when you come
out of the pool!"

"What about the wig?" I said.

"We can use it later. In the Marie Antoinette sequence."

There was a good deal of kissing.

It was not till I got back to my office that I remembered
that, to the best of my knowledge, there *was* no Marie Antoinette sequence in the picture.

*   *   *   *   *

Cathy's accent, unnoticeable and to some (me) utterly
charming, has worried André. It has worried some of our
"Guest Stars." It has worried the Sound Department (notori-
ous worriers). In point of fact, as her dialogue consists mainly

of "Yes!" "Yes, yes!" "Yes, yes, *yes!*" "Wow!" "Yum!" "Yum! Yum!" and "Goody!" there is really no problem at all.

I have found in my brief tenure as Head of the Studio that most of the day-to-day problems that arise can be solved if one retains sufficient objectivity to ignore them until the inevitable *new* set of problems appears, automatically erasing the former set of problems, and these, *too,* will solve themselves if one simply awaits the *next* set of problems. . . .

 *   *   *   *   *

Acting on the possibility that there yet *might* be a Marie Antoinette sequence in the film, I have written the first (and, obviously, last) joke of my life. It is a pun, really. The King of France is berating his wife for her grotesque bad taste in lovers. I had thought it might be amusing for Cathy to reply: *"Shack-up à son goût."*

I mentioned it (with studied casualness) to André. He, following my above-stated precept (which he has obviously known all along), is patiently waiting for it to go away.

On the other hand, we *do* have the Petit Trianon already constructed on the back lot. It would be a simple matter to move the contract players out for a day or two. And, if I do say so myself, it's a pretty good joke. Also we could get to use the wig. Which would certainly make Sidney happy.

There is something contagious about the madness of this business. And power, I have discovered, is pretty heady stuff.

I press the buzzer (one of a series) on my desk. I hear my own voice saying, in tones of brisk command, "I have decided there will be a Marie Antoinette sequence. Please inform all departments."

Thank God I am not President of the United States.

I would have pressed the "Button" at least four times in the past week. Just for the hell of it.

2

This, to return to reality and the present tense, is a suicide note.

I have been rereading my production log. But it is getting late.

It is now four o'clock in the afternoon.

Mr. Smith and (I presume) Miss Garbo have been safely ensconced in the Beverly Hills Hotel.

Cathy is crazed.

She has been in and out of this office seventeen times modeling various garments, seeking my advice on what might be suitable for her to wear on this, the evening of her triumph.

I should have suggested widow's weeds. But we are, of course, unmarried.

We have settled upon something enormously sedate.

Sidney is even now doing her hair.

*   *   *   *   *

My picture has garnered twenty-seven nominations.

I do not seriously believe that it has anything whatsoever to do with the merit (nonexistent) of the film. It is simply a matter of anti-youth backlash. The average age of the voting members of the Academy is fifty-six. All our male performers have haircuts. All our ladies look as if they had just emerged from the bath.

In its way, my predecessor's statement about "middle-aged persons groping each other on the screen" has backfired.

There are, apparently, vast numbers of persons over thirty in the country. And (judging from the box-office statements) they clearly enjoy watching their contemporaries "grope" each other on the screen.

Anyone with four eyes (most of my generation wear glasses) can *see* that Gregory Peck is more beautiful than Dennis Hopper; Elizabeth more divine ánd womanly than . . . why is it that no one can ever *remember* the names of the younger female "stars"?

I append my Form Sheet for tonight's Awards.

BEST PICTURE (*Almost a shoo-in; it was the only major film made in Hollywood this year, and the Academy is usually quite loyal in these matters.*)

BEST ACTOR: Tracy Steele. (*His competition is slight. A Japanese, a Czech, and two bearded youths who are not even members of the Academy.*)

BEST ACTRESS: Cathy. (*After her unfortunate— for Johnny—appearance on the Carson Show, her Oscar is a foregone conclusion.*)

BEST SUPPORTING MALE AND FEMALE (*Up for grabs. All our "Guest Stars" insisted on below-the-title billing, so it looks like a pretty close race between Frank & Richard & Burt & Kirk & Greg. And on the distaff side, Deborah & Natalie & Kim & Elizabeth & Shirley.*)

BEST DIRECTOR: André. (*He has already won the Director's Guild Award. What could go wrong?*)

BEST SCREENPLAY ADAPTED FROM AN-OTHER MEDIUM (*In the bag.*)

* * * * *

The Screenwriter is with me even now. He is working on his acceptance speech. The other writing Award, for a Story Written Directly for the Screen, is, alas, beyond our grasp. Some long-haired twenty-two-year-old seems to have that one wrapped up. The Screenwriter, having finished his speech, picks up the *Hollywood Reporter.*

"I'll be a son of a bitch," he says. "I think the kid is my *son.* At least I have one with the same name. His mother got

custody, of course. Quite correctly. We had lunch last year in
New York. He looked awful and asked me if I thought he
should try to get a job in movies. I told him to get his hair cut
and forget it. I was pretty drunk, as I remember it. I'll be a
son of a bitch. I kind of hope the kid wins."

The rest of the awards are technical and of no interest
to anyone except the winners and their immediate families.

But they are all *mine!*

My friend the propman assures me of that.

It looks like a sweep.

* * * * *

The Screenwriter has gone. We spoke for a while of
Tracy Steele's drinking. We are both terribly worried about
him.

* * * * *

Tracy has come and gone. He dropped by to check out
his speech and express concern about the Screenwriter's drinking. He is, we agree, an extremely talented man and certainly
capable of better and more important things. If there were
only some way we could help him with his problem.

* * * * *

I hope to God we can all get through tonight without
a really appalling calamity.

* * * * *

Where the *hell* is Cathy?
I should love
I should dearly love
Just one more glorious
Before the wards and my farture
Have steamer tickets in desk.

God I am so drunk. Those two bastards. Really worried about them. Nice guys. Good friends would not play
practical jokes like Ed Max Ed. But they drink too much
    Me my liver doesn't matter will soon me dead
    this is a
    cathy I love you
    note . . .

Chapter FOURTEEN

1

Because of the time difference in New York, the Academy Award Ceremonies start in Los Angeles at the preposterous hour of 6 P.M.

Tracy and the Screenwriter were seated at the bar in Tracy's suite. It was then a few minutes before five.

"I'm really worried about Harve," Tracy said. "He's drinking much too much for his own good." He held out his glass, which Tiger Wilson automatically refilled.

"I wasn't going to say anything," the Screenwriter said, "but I'm a little worried myself." He too held out his glass. "I wish there was some way we could help him with his Problem."

"The main thing is to get him through tonight."

Tracy was immaculately dressed in white tie and tails. The Screenwriter wore his usual costume. While it is not one of the Commandments, writers are generally well advised to eschew evening dress. The standard reply *used* to be: If I wished to look like a saxophone-player, I would learn to play the saxophone.

As hardly anyone plays the saxophone any more, this remark is no longer as relevant as it once was. The Screenwriter, in fact, looked rather "trendy." Had he known it, the idea would have shocked him to the marrow.

* * * * *

Meanwhile, in another part of town, his son, locks newly shorn, was trying on his first (rented) tuxedo. "Typical," his female companion was saying. "One lousy Nomination and suddenly you're part of the Establishment!" The Screenwriter's son adjusted his tie in the mirror. "If I wished," he replied with some dignity, "to look like a member of The Grateful Dead I would learn to play an electric guitar!"

There is a French observation that, roughly translated, means: the more things change, the more they stay the same.

As the Screenwriter's son had majored in "Contemporary Relevance" for the six months before he had dropped out of college, he would not have understood it anyway.

* * * * *

"It's after five," Tracy said. "Do you think we should go over and see if Harve is all right?"

"Absolutely," the Screenwriter said. "The only thing is, with his problem and all, I hate to drink in front of him. Why don't we just have a quick one here for the road and then off we go."

When they got to Harvey's office twenty minutes later, Harvey was gone.

"Good old Harve," Tracy said. "I knew he wouldn't let the side down!"

They had one more quick one in Harvey's honor and then took off for the Music Center in the Screenwriter's Rolls Royce.

2

Harvey finished his suicide note.

He folded it carefully into an envelope. He placed the

envelope in his out box, scribbling some of Cathy's names on the front in a shaky hand.

At a given stage of drunkenness, when it is too late for retreat, there is only one course left open. It is occasionally possible to "drink yourself sober again." At least this is a theory widely held in certain ever-narrowing circles.

It was, probably, with this in mind that Harvey took a fresh bottle of vodka from the bar and lurched out of the office.

A few minutes later the Master of Properties, in white tie and tails, found the Head of the Studio wandering through the parking lot in his white bush jacket, clutching his bottle.

He took Harvey gently by the arm.

"Mr. Bernstein," he said. "You're pushing yourself too hard."

"Awards," Harvey said.

"Come on," the Master of Properties said. "I'll give you a lift. It would be a great honor, sir."

He helped Harvey into his Lincoln (while everyone else had been given free Mustangs, the Master of Properties had received a Continental. Ralph Nader to the contrary, the Ford Motor Company *occasionally* knows what it's doing).

They arrived at the Music Center and entered through the stage door. The Master of Properties was a Past President of the Union and was held (rightly) in the highest esteem by his fellows.

He led Harvey deftly through the crowds backstage to the prop room. Once inside, he locked the door.

He and Harvey were *roughly* the same size. Anyhow, they were the same height, and had Harvey been subjected to a few months more of Felix's cooking they would probably have been of almost equal girth.

The Master of Properties removed his tailcoat, undid his white tie, and slipped out of his stiff shirt and his trousers.

"Just give me your bush jacket, Mr. Bernstein," he said, "and your trousers. That's it. On a night like this, sir, I know you will wish to be appropriately attired." He put on the bush jacket and the trousers. "I'll be waiting just outside the door if you have any trouble with the tie."

Harvey murmured his thanks.

The door closed behind the Master of Properties. Harvey glanced at his watch, trying desperately to bring his eyes into focus. It was just six o'clock. These things always started late. And besides, BEST PICTURE was always the last of the Awards. He had plenty of time. In the interests of trying to sober up, he had another (longish) drink from the neck of the bottle. Then he removed the rest of his clothes and passed out on a pile of sandbags which were stored in the prop room against fire, flood, or some other unforeseeable act of God.

3

The Special Security Guard was very young and very, very eager. He had just caught a glimpse of Bob Hope (in person) and his sense of dedication-to-duty was running high.

He grabbed the Master of Properties by the arm.

"You a writer?" he asked.

His instructions had been explicit. The only persons permitted backstage without evening dress were writers. (None of the twelve men with Mr. Hope had been wearing evening dress. But they *had* been writers.)

The Master of Properties was not used to this sort of treatment. Also, *his* sense of dedication to duty was running high. He was there to guard the person and protect the dignity of the Head of His Studio.

He made the mistake of swinging at the Security Guard who had recently completed a six-week course in unarmed combat and riot prevention.

To the everlasting glory of the Property Department, it took three additional Security Guards and two regular Los Angeles cops to subdue and eject him.

There was hell to pay afterward, of course. The Union demanding and getting a formal apology from everyone concerned.

But by that time, naturally, it was too late.

4

Cathy arrived with Sidney at six-fifteen. They had spent the latter part of the afternoon trying on wigs. They had finally decided to use her own hair. ("Harve," Sidney said, "would want it that way.") Fortunately, the elaborate hairdo they had created was blown to pieces in Sidney's convertible (he, too, had made a deal with the Ford Motor Company), and she looked just sensational.

Her entrance was delayed for almost half an hour by the Press. There was a television interview in the lobby. That took more time. She and Tracy Steele were photographed embracing from a number of angles.

Tracy had, through years of experience, got the autograph thing down to almost 1.5 seconds per signature. Cathy, who had lately begun to feel a responsibility toward her "fans," took 16 seconds per autograph. Being careful to get the spelling of the name of the person to whom she was signing the program correct, and making sure to dot the "i" in Lovibond and cross the "t" in Lamont.

Mr. Hope was just finishing his monologue when she and Tracy were finally able to make their way to their seats.

Felix was resplendent in his tails.

Veronica X's outfit had caused considerable comment.

"Dior?" the man from *Women's Wear Daily* had asked.

"Frederick's of Hollywood," she had replied.

"Where's Harvey?" Cathy whispered to Tracy.

"Probably backstage somewhere," Tracy said. "Making sure that everything's under control."

5

"And here to present the Award for Best Screenplay Written Directly for the Screen is . . . Miss Alice *Faye!*"

The applause was tumultuous.

Miss Faye looked great.

After a moment or two of suspense and the wrong cards which had been originally handed to her having been straightened out, Miss Faye read the name of the winner.

The young man with the newly cut hair and the rented tuxedo was shy but really very pleased.

In the wings the Screenwriter broke away from the photographers and dashed back out onto the stage and threw his arms around his son.

"Jesus, Dad," the kid said, "everybody else is in evening clothes. You look lousy. Also, you need a haircut."

"You little shit," the Screenwriter said.

It was not exactly the ending of *Love Story,* and neither of them cried. But they became pretty good friends afterward anyway.

6

The words "Alice Faye" over the backstage loudspeakers brought Harvey Bernstein to life with a start. He had been dreaming about Cathy and the last thing he could *really* (at that moment) remember was being led to the shower on that long-ago night in the apartment in Astoria.

He rose. Sort of.

Sandbags are not the greatest thing in the world to pass out on.

He was pleased to discover that he was still wearing his glasses. Through them he was able to discern the outlines of a vodka bottle.

Everything was in slow motion.

He dimly heard Tracy Steele's acceptance speech. Very short. Very dignified. Received with tremendous applause.

Then Cathy.

He suddenly knew where he was and what he had to do. He could not let her down. This was her night of triumph. It had been his plan (everyone, no matter how remotely connected with the making of a motion picture, always prepares his Academy Award acceptance in his mind), when called upon to receive the Best Picture Award, to make a brief speech of thanks and then call His People—he had in his madness begun to think of them that way—onto the stage to share the moment.

He heard his own name boom over the speakers.

Filled with love, vodka, passion, sweat, tears, and a (perhaps) not unmisplaced sense of history, he lunged to his feet, flung open the prop room door, and made his way toward the brightly lighted stage.

Nobody, not even the security guards, made a move to stop him.

There have been a number of extraordinary moments in the history of Academy Award Presentations. But almost never before had the Producer of the Best Picture of the Year strode onto the stage, in full view of several hundred million persons (the event was being televised, live, by Telstar) to receive his award, wearing only his glasses and one sock (beige).

In the auditorium Veronica X clutched Felix's hand.

"That Mr. Bernstein!" she said. "You never know what he going to do *next!*"

What Mr. Bernstein did next was grab his Oscar, blurt out the word "suicide," and run blindly for the train.

Or, in this case, the boat.

PROLOGUE

(CONCLUDED)

This is a suicide note.

I mean, *really*, this time—no kidding around!

The worst of it was, apparently (I have only the word of the hundred and thirty or so million persons who actually *saw* the actual *live* actual broadcast *itself*—the instant replay was, I am told, instantly edited to a "waistshot"), I had been dreaming there, on the sand bags, of Cathy.

Words fail me.

"THE BIGGEST THING IN SHOW BUSINESS" was the unfortunate way *The Daily Variety* chose to phrase it. *Women's Wear Daily* mentioned (discreetly) only my beige sock.

*   *   *   *   *

This is a suicide note.

*   *   *   *   *

I have become, according to the newspapers that Captain Sigbjørn brings to my cabin at each port of call (he has, I believe, penetrated my disguise—a false beard purloined from the prop room at the Music Center, used, normally, in their occasional and, I fear, indifferently sung and performed productions of *Rigoletto*), an object of female sexual fantasy unequaled since Charles "Sonny" Wisecarver, an eleven-year-old sex maniac of the late '30's, named as correspondent in forty-three divorce actions.

$$* \quad * \quad * \quad * \quad * \quad *$$

I ventured up to the top deck last night. It was the third night out.

I toyed with the notion of jumping.

Then did so.

$$* \quad * \quad * \quad * \quad * \quad *$$

Splash.

Bull shit!

All this is just part of a best-selling novel that he *is trying to write.*

He *would no more commit suicide than* I *would.*

I found his note and met the ship in Panama City.

Which is not where we are.

If you wish to communicate with H.B., or C.L.L.L.L., try New York. L.A. Vegas. Miami. or Here.

Choose one.